Trust the Wind

Trust the Wind

By Claire Crafts

Trust the Wind

Copyright © 2018 by Claire Crafts

Edited by Lorna Collins
Cover design by Larry K. Collins
I

ISBN-13: 978-1717541918
ISBN-10: 1717541917
ASIN: B07CQY67Q8

Contents

Dedication

~~To my writing parents, Lorna and Larry, without whom this dream never would have come true~~

*"You can trust the wind, breathe the air.
There's a place you're meant to be, and you're already
there."*

Lyrics by David Friedman

Chapter 1

The cool wind tickled my nose and blew my streaked blonde hair over my face, tangling it in the yellow grass. As I lay in the stillness of late summer, a sketchbook abandoned on the ground beside me, my eyes wandered past the tall trees that surrounded the meadow and rested on the sky. Bluer than the ocean, it had been my second home. At the thought of home, *my old home*, I corrected myself, my heart winced. For a moment, I allowed myself to miss the salty smell of the California breeze. It had once cooled my bedroom during hot summer nights, where warm weather rarely changed year-round. For just a moment, I immersed myself in all the memories and accompanying pain of what I had lost. But I let it go in the Montana wind, for the time being, at least. The wind was my constant companion, and I knew it would return.

A loud buzzing broke me from my reverie, the kind of buzzing even a California girl would recognize. I scrambled up from the bed of grass and hastily took a few steps away, shaking my hair out at the same time.

I heard a faint chuckle behind me. "It's just a bee. Lots of things in this neck of the woods can do far more damage to you than a tiny bumble bee can."

I turned to find the owner of the voice. "Who are you?" My heart jumped a little at the sight of someone my own age, a cute someone in fact, as he casually leaned against an old fence.

"Emily, come back to the house." My mom's voice rang from the kitchen window. "We have guests."

I grimaced. Mom, as always, had impeccable timing. I smiled apologetically and turned to go, too shy to say anything and ruin the moment.

"My name is Lucas, by the way. Nice to meet you, Emily?" His friendly hazel eyes questioned me.

I nodded my head. "Nice to meet you too, Lucas." I gave him a half-smile.

I turned and jogged quickly toward the small hill topped with a large two-story house, a house I was supposed to call home. As I ran, I imagined him watching me. So, I ran faster. The wind I loved rushed through my tangled hair. I could almost picture myself with my team again, a soccer ball dancing at my feet, breaking away from the defenders, and hearing the crisp sound of the ball hitting the net.

Then I was alone again, atop the hill my sister had christened "Dungeon Hill" while my team played hundreds of miles away. My heart winced in the fashion becoming all too familiar, *my old team.*

I quietly let myself in the kitchen door and heard my parents talking to our guest in the living room.

I recognized my mom speaking first. "Yes, we moved here because of Chris's promotion. I saw it as a perfect opportunity for the kids. Life was too hectic with all their sports and activities in California. They never had a chance to stop and enjoy living. It became overwhelming. We needed a change."

I peeked in and saw my mom sigh and glance at my dad. "We realized with all the activities, life was passing us by. We only have one year until Lydia, she's our oldest daughter, leaves for college—"

Dad joined in to finish her thought. "We had visited Yellowstone a couple years back. When my company asked me to relocate here—we did."

Mom laughed. "All our friends thought we were crazy."

"It still feels pretty crazy." Dad laughed with her.

I heard our guest's voice for the first time. "Do you regret it? You've only been here for a month and a half, so it might be too early to make a judgment." His tone was soft and low, melodically soothing. "I apologize for not introducing myself sooner. My son told me the old Carson house had been sold, but I didn't realize how quickly you would move in."

"No problem. And no, we don't regret it." My dad exchanged glances with my mom again. "It's been a hard adjustment for the kids, especially Lydia. But once they get over their homesickness, I think they're going to like it here."

"As much as we all miss our friends," Mom said in a wistful tone, "we needed this change. The kids just weren't—blooming. It's the word I use. They had everything, but they weren't embracing the joy of life."

I couldn't help but snort and roll my eyes at my mother's dramatic way of talking about our "new life," but I gave away my hidden position.

"Emily, you can stop hiding and come in. Mr. Wright, this is my second daughter, Emily."

"Nice to meet you, Emily. And please, all of you, call me Michael."

"Emily always teases me about my descriptions of how the kids weren't 'blooming.' She says I'm too dramatic." My mom smiled at me and squeezed my hand.

Mom always treated me as if I were slightly fragile, sensitive maybe. She didn't quite understand me, like she did Lydia, who was practically the same person as my mother, just in teenage form.

"My son should be here soon. He decided to walk from our place a couple miles up the road." Michael chuckled. "Crazy kid." But I could sense the pride in his voice.

"Speaking of kids—" My father raised his voice and called up the stairs. "Lydia and Liam, please come down. This is the second time I've asked you."

Liam ran out of Lydia's room giggling. "Lydia's on the phone with her *boyfriend*." He mimicked Lydia on the phone, "Finn, Finn, oh I love you soooo much."

"Shut up, idiot. You know I don't say that."

I could tell from Lydia's expression, as she stalked down the stairs after Liam, she was in a foul mood. "So, Mr. Wright, I take it you heard my mother's blooming speech. Did you notice its rehearsed nature? I'll tell you why. It's the same speech she gave to our family, friends, and neighbors back in California." Lydia deliberately placed one foot after another down the staircase, emphasizing her anger with each step. Her fiery gaze remained unwaveringly on poor Mr. Wright. "But I'll also tell you the real reason we are here having this pleasant conversation in the middle of nowhere. Three words: Dad. Got. Promoted." She reached the bottom of the staircase and shook the man's hand as we watched in horrified silence. "It's been so nice meeting you."

Lydia left the room. We heard her banging around in the kitchen.

Dad dared to speak. "I apologize for my daughter's behavior. This transition has been the hardest for her, although it does not excuse her outburst."

My mother pushed my brother forward. "This is our youngest, Liam. Dear, meet Mr. Wright."

Leave it to Mom to cover up an awkward situation by turning my brother's cute little grin on him.

"Nice to meet you." Michael smiled warmly at my brother's enthusiastic handshake.

A knock at the door interrupted the introductions.

"This must be your son." Mom motioned for me to answer it.

I walked the short distance and opened the door. Summer's cool night breeze washed over me, sending shivers down my spine as I finally recognized who stood in the doorway. He laughed at what must have been the surprise on my face.

"Lucas?" I finally stuttered out.

He didn't look nearly as surprised as I did. "Hey."

From a distance, I could hear my mother calling me to bring him inside. But his laugh was too infectious for me to really register anything else.

"Well aren't you going to let me in?"

Of course, I did.

Chapter 2

"That was a great stunt you pulled tonight." I turned to Lydia with my eyebrows raised as I pulled on my pajamas.

"Oh come on. Don't tell me you weren't thinking it." Lydia adjusted the curtains between our beds.

"Yeah, but I don't go running my mouth off in front of Mom and Dad and some poor stranger."

"This whole situation sucks. Our parents are being jerks about it. And you just mouse around miserably trying not to step on toes. I have taken it upon myself to fix it." With her dramatic pronouncement, she settled into her bed.

I snorted. "You did a fantastic job tonight. Mom and Dad are so mad I don't even know what they're going to do to you tomorrow."

"One step at a time, young one. Let the master do her work."

I couldn't help but laugh. "It might be hard for the master to do her work once she's been grounded without her phone or computer for a month."

Lydia mumbled to herself and turned from her back to face me. "Let's talk about something else."

I yawned and grabbed my phone to see what texts I had missed. *Only one from Cora.* A familiar ache tugged at my heart. *God, I miss home so much. Just ignore it and don't think about California.* I shoved the thoughts away and put my phone down to return to the conversation. "What do you want to talk about?"

Her mischievous smile was never a good sign.

"Lucas."

I felt my cheeks heat up. "Um, what about him?"

"You are one lovesick puppy." My sister shook her head.

"I don't know what you are talking about." I rolled over to face the wall, so she couldn't see my expression from her bed across the room and ignored the repeated *dings* from my phone.

She laughed. "You have all the signs. Distant expression, quick laughter at his terrible jokes, glancing at him when you think he isn't looking..."

I tried to ignore the thumping of my heart even as she spoke. "Don't be ridiculous. I only met him today."

"That's all it takes sometimes."

"Goodnight, Lydia." I decided it was time to end the conversation before it could become any more awkward.

"I think he likes you, too, you know."

I refused to respond, knowing my voice would betray my true feelings.

Chapter 3

The next morning, I woke early and sat on the front steps in my pajamas, shivering in the crisp mountain air. Two small fawns frolicked in the meadow, all the while staying close to their mother. This was one thing I enjoyed about being in Montana, these summer mornings. The world was so quiet I could practically hear the steady thumping of my heart. All I had to do was look out my window to see deer grazing in the yellowish green grass or squirrels running around in the tall pine trees.

I let my head rest against the post, but my eyes were drawn once more to the sky. My lids drifted shut until a familiar voice awakened me.

"Nice nap?"

I woke up startled but couldn't suppress a yawn. Embarrassed, I hugged my arms tightly to my chest. "Uh, yeah. You woke me up, though."

He laughed. "It's a little early to be taking a nap."

I had to smile.

My mother's voice ruined the moment. "Lucas. I'm surprised to see you here so early this morning."

He reached down and pulled me up from the porch steps, and then followed me into the house. "Yes, Mrs. Lawrence, I think I left my jacket, and I was wondering if you had it here."

My sister walked in and gave me a knowing smile.

"No, I didn't see any jacket last night after you left."

Lydia sipped her coffee innocently.

"Okay. Um, well I guess I'd better get back then." Lucas flushed and headed toward the door.

I walked him out to the steps. He stopped and turned around suddenly. "Hey, are you doing anything today?"

"No." I hoped he couldn't see the anticipation and excitement in my expression.

"Would you, uh, want me to show you around or something?"

"Sure." I tried to sound casual.

"See you later then, I guess." I watched him walk away and then turned to go inside.

My sister stood in the doorway. Her mischievous grin stopped me.

"Did you just get asked on a date?"

"Don't be ridiculous." I turned red and quickly escaped into the house.

~ ~ ~

The minutes seemed to pass unbearably slowly. Finally giving up on the pretense of reading, I closed my book and pushed my nose against the window. I watched the fog from my breath form a small circle on the glass and slowly fade again and again. Yelling coming from my room distracted me from the monotony.

Lydia came stomping down the stairs clutching her computer and phone. "I am not submitting to your tyranny. I have a life, you know. And it's not here. So it looks like my phone and computer will be necessary to keep up. Besides, you know as well as I do that I have dozens of college essays to write."

My mother followed closely behind, her cheeks revealing her anger. "Stop being so dramatic. Your life is here now, whether you like it or not. Hand over the computer and phone now, or they will be taken away longer. You can use the desktop downstairs for your college essays."

"Dramatic? *You* want to talk to *me* about being dramatic? I seem to recall someone telling everyone we know we were moving halfway across the country because her kids weren't blooming."

"Lydia, please. I don't want to make this a bigger problem than it already is."

"A bigger argument than it already is? I don't know if it's possible. You know what I consider to be one of the biggest problems? Moms who don't take their children's lives and opinions into consideration when making major family decisions instead caring about selfish things like Dad's big new title and where she wants to live."

Mom's cheeks grew dangerously red. She now stood facing Lydia in the middle of the living room. "I will not take this sass from you. I am done with this conversation. Do what I say before your consequences get worse."

"Actually, I'm going to follow the example you have set and be selfish and uncaring about what my other family members think or want me to do." She turned for her room, slammed the door, and locked it behind her.

As I quietly let myself out of the house, the sound of Mom's angry retort followed me out the door. During arguments like this, I considered the safest place was the farthest possible away.

As the days in our new home had passed, I'd often found myself alone, hiding in the meadow.

When I was by myself, I missed California the most. Clashes between Lydia and Mom had not been unheard of, they were fewer and farther between before we moved. I guess strong personalities like theirs were destined to fight, but back then, I had Cora to talk to.

I can't even think about Cora right now. If I let myself miss her, I'll get sucked into missing everything about California. I live here now, and I have to move on. Somehow, my determination didn't match the aching in my chest.

I took a deep breath, stood up from the grass, and gently began to pluck small wildflowers from the surrounding ground. My thoughts drifted to a much more pleasant topic: Lucas.

Suddenly, burning humiliation rose like bile in my throat. *I forgot to ask him where we were meeting.* So much for a nice day.

Instead, I sat on the fence, swinging my legs back and forth. It was almost therapeutic, the swinging movement, eerily calming in a way. I stared out into the woods, knowing I should be a little frightened of the absolute wildness beyond. But somehow, I wasn't.

My somber contemplation was interrupted by a tap on my shoulder. I jumped off the fence and spun around. "Who? Oh, hi, Lucas. I didn't hear you walk up."

He grinned. "Scared ya."

"You *surprised* me. There's a difference," I responded with a smile as ran my fingers through my hair.

"Well, are you ready to go?" He turned and started walking the other way.

Startled, I wordlessly jumped off the fence and followed him.

Chapter 4

An hour later, I was panting. "Are we there yet?" We had tramped through thick forest for what felt like forever without saying a word, and I was beginning to get frustrated.

"Typical for a California girl to get tired before we're even halfway there."

I felt my face flame with anger. "I play soccer, you know. I'm out of shape from not playing in a while, but even so, I could run faster than you with my eyes closed."

He scoffed. "Soccer? What's the point? You might be faster than me at a sprint, but I could run for miles without stopping."

I tried to control the defensive anger in my tone. "You're so isolated out here in your hermit hole. I bet you've never even seen a soccer game."

He turned and faced me. "I have a TV, you know. I'm not so isolated I don't know what's happening. I just know I'd *never* want to be a part of the life you're used to." His eyes darkened. For a moment, I was frightened.

"Geez, no need to get so upset. Sorry if I said something to upset you." Sarcasm managed to seep into my last words.

His eyes softened. "I'm sorry. I shouldn't have taken my anger out on you. Rough morning."

I forgave him easily when he looked at me with his hurt-puppy expression. "I shouldn't have retaliated."

We walked a little farther in silence.

"We'll be there soon."

I was content to follow him quietly for a few minutes more before my curiosity got the best of me. "What exactly do you have against the life I used to live or whatever you referred to a minute ago?"

I was starting to think I had offended him again when he finally responded. "I just know some people who became so immersed in all the business of the big city they sort of lost track of themselves and everybody they cared about. Needless to say, I'm not a huge fan of the outside world anymore." He looked at me sideways. "Then again, people consider me somewhat hermitish because I'm content with these woods and the few friends I have."

How come a guy like Lucas only has a few friends? I could tell from his tense shoulders the subject upset him. "We just met yesterday. You don't have to talk about this if you don't want to."

"It's fine." His uncomfortable expression clearly told me it was not fine.

Why is he acting so awkward? "Um, are you sure?"

He let out a sigh. "Yeah. Sorry if I'm acting weird. It's been a while since I've hung out with someone new who's my own age."

This kid just gets more and more interesting. "No, you're fine. I understand. It's weird for me too." *I am in a different state, after all.*

We walked along in silence for a while, the only sound the crunching of leaves and grass beneath our feet.

He broke the silence suddenly. "You're from California, so you probably know better than I do what's considered normal."

I nodded. "Well, maybe."

"Is it weird that I never wanna leave this place?"

My jaw dropped. "You never want to leave here?"

He shrugged. "Honestly, I don't think people who live away from the world in the wildernesses like this who have it wrong. Everyone out there in the world has it backward."

I fumbled for words. "What? What do you mean we have it backward?" I was so caught up in my own confusion I almost ran into him when he stopped.

"We're here."

Then there were no more words. The wind rushed over my body, filling up all of my senses. I felt like I had found myself alone on a stage with hundreds of people staring at me, and I couldn't remember what to say. Or like when I wordlessly stared into a cute boy's eyes, mesmerized by his closeness and the pounding of my heart, and I realized he was just saying. "Hi." It was the same smallness, humility, even stupidity I felt when looking at something far greater than myself, the realization I had been missing something all along.

"I understand why we walked for so long," I whispered. The sun sparkled off the water like small rainbows, and the roar as it crashed down the descent of a rocky slide overpowered my senses. Then the colors assaulted me. The green of the moss and overhanging trees was more vibrant than I'd seen before in my life, and the small flowers left over from the bloom of spring glowed with tenacity, which had allowed them to survive so long.

Lucas pointed at the large brown form distantly in the river downstream, and all the joy in my heart from my surroundings felt like it had been punched out of me. "Is that a—?" I had to yell for my voice to be heard over the crashing water.

"Grizzly?" He finished my thought and nodded his head. "Yeah."

I clutched his arm and automatically stepped back from the overlook on which we had paused. "We have to go. Now. It's not safe."

"Aww, he's not even full-grown. Besides, he already knows we're here. We're past any danger." He leaned down so I could understand his words.

Air still had not entered my lungs.

"Breathe, Ems. We won't go any closer."

All of a sudden, I was aware of how near he was, and the ease with which the nickname rolled off his tongue.

"Ems?" My lips still barely made a sound.

"Yeah, my sister's name is Emily. I always used to call her that."

"You have a sister?"

His eyes darkened again. "I don't want to talk about her right now. It'll ruin the moment." He was quiet for a second and then looked at me with something close to brotherly affection. "Would you mind releasing my arm? I'd appreciate it if my blood was allowed back to my heart."

I quickly released him, but I could feel my face reddening to the soft laughter from under his breath. He took a few steps closer to the edge with a grin still etched on his face.

My irritation got the best of me. "You can be kind of a pain sometimes," I shouted over the roaring, which surrounded us.

"A nice kind of pain, I hope?" He turned and looked back at me curiously, almost eagerly.

I couldn't prevent the smile. "I guess you're a nice pain, whatever it's supposed to mean."

The familiar breeze tugged at my hair and tickled my nose till I laughed. The wind always seemed to join me at moments like these, when I was perfectly, blissfully happy.

~ ~ ~

We sat in the long grass of the overlook for a long time. We didn't talk much, mostly because it was easier than shouting or reading each other's lips over the sound of the waterfall. The quiet was nice in a way. Neither of us felt any need to fill in the empty space because there was none. The lonesomeness of living in the middle of nowhere provided time for contemplation, and I was becoming comfortable with the sound of my own voice in my head. There wasn't much else to do. I was beginning to realize the loud world hadn't left much time for me to think, and all my thoughts, which had been ignored for so long, finally were beginning to appear.

He repositioned himself so he was sitting right next to me, our hips touching. "What are you thinking about?" His eyes locked with mine.

I looked away from the intensity, gazing instead at the waterfall. "Thinking about thinking, I guess. People here don't talk very much."

He nodded and was quiet for a moment. "Maybe it's because a lot of the things we think can better be expressed in actions, not words."

"You are very wise for someone our age, you know. I don't think I've ever met anyone quite like you." I said the words before thinking, not realizing the how cheesy they might sound.

He laughed it off. "Maybe it's just because I have a lot of time to think. While you spent your adolescence chattering away with your friends, I spent it out in this forest, alone except for my thoughts and the grizzlies."

I smiled at his humor, but inwardly I was thinking of my friends, thinking of Cora, the friend I missed the most.

"You miss them, your friends, don't you?"

It was funny how his words so accurately described my thoughts even before I understood them myself. "Yes, I do. But there definitely are things I don't miss." The achy feeling in my chest slowly began to creep in at the thought of what I was missing. I stood up suddenly. "Do you want to start heading back?"

He shrugged. "As you wish."

At the familiar words, I turned around and laughed. "*The Princess Bride*? Really?"

"It doesn't get any better." He laughed, too.

We talked about movies on our entire return trip. When we had finally reached my house, he casually turned to me. "So, was it a good day?"

Maybe I imagined the hopefulness in his tone. "Yes." My response contained a bit too much enthusiasm.

He didn't seem to notice. "Wanna do it again sometime?"

"Sure." I barely contained the smile, which seemed to burst from my whole being.

Chapter 5

"Hah, I win. Again." I jumped up from my chair in a victory dance, sending my cards flying everywhere.

Liam sulked back in his chair. "It's just because I went easy on you. Rematch."

The doorbell interrupted my dance. "Oh, it must be Lucas." I grabbed my phone from the table and headed toward the door. "Bye, Liam."

"Wait what?" He stood up in indignation. "You promised we could play three games. We just finished one. *And* you probably cheated, so you owe me another one."

I gasped in mock shock. "I cannot believe you would accuse me of such crimes. When have I ever cheated at card games?"

He laughed. "Um, like every time. Dad refuses to play with you anymore because you've gotten caught so many times."

"Whatever. I actually have to go now, though. So, bye." I tried to continue out of the room.

"Mom," Liam yelled. "Emily promised to play three games with me, and now she's leaving after one."

I spun around. "Are you seriously tattling on me for this?"

"Mom." He outright ignored me.

"What's going on?" Mom appeared from the laundry room drying her hands.

"I have to go. Lucas is waiting outside for me."

"Lucas is here?"

"Yes." I sighed in frustration. "I already told you we were going on a hike today."

"Mom, she promised to play three games with me," Liam whined.

She silenced him with a look. "You're going on a hike again?"

"Yes." I cut her off. "I'm leaving now."

"Not a very creative guy," she muttered under her breath.

"I heard you." I turned and left the house. I closed the door behind me and gave a huge sigh of relief when I heard it latch.

"Hi." He grinned goofily at me.

I smiled back, distracted by the way the wind rushed through his hair. "Hi."

"What took you so long?"

"Liam was mad because I wasn't going to play another game with him."

"I don't have those problems since I'm the only kid at home now."

"Lucky." I laughed as we began to walk down the stairs.

He looked at me with a bemused smile. "Not really, actually."

I didn't know how to respond, so I changed the subject. "So, where are we going today?"

"It's a surprise."

I had to walk extra fast to keep up with his long strides. "Can I have a hint?"

"You probably haven't been there anyway."

"True, but I still want a hint."

We stopped at the beginning of a barely perceptible trailhead.

"It requires a lot of walking to get there."

I laughed and followed.

After what felt like hours, we finally arrived in a small clearing. "No waterfalls this time, huh?" I made a sad attempt a joke.

He seemed unperturbed and unaffected by my humor. "Nah. This time we are looking at a tree."

I raised my eyebrows. "A tree? We could have walked three steps from my house and found as many trees as we wanted."

"This, Emily Lawrence, is a special tree."

Oh boy.

"This tree is one of the oldest trees in our entire area. It's a couple hundred years old." He gazed up at the tree, towering above all the others surrounding it.

"It's actually pretty cool."

"Always the tone of surprise. Don't you trust me by now on these hikes?"

"I dunno." I tried for a casual voice.

"What?" He laughed. "Why not?"

"I'm kidding." I exhaled with a giggle. "If I didn't trust you, I would never be following you around the Montana wilderness."

He smiled. "Do you want to sit down for a few minutes before we head back?"

I breathed a sigh of relief. "Thank God you asked."

We sat down with our backs against the tree. *This is surprisingly comfortable. And I am surprisingly very content right now.* I turned to look at Lucas. "Hey, can I ask you a random question?"

"Sure."

"Why did you ask me to hang out the other day? I mean like right after we met?" My heart thumped in trepidation, hoping he would respond the way I wanted him to.

"You reminded me of my sister," he responded simply.

My stomach fell. *Not the answer I wanted to hear from the guy I like.* Another thought came unbidden. "Wait, is this the same sister you don't like talking about?" *This is just great. I remind him of the family member who makes him upset.*

He smiled a bit. "No. I mean how my sister was before she left."

I was dying to ask more questions, but his tone signified he wanted the conversation to end there. I stood up and brushed the dirt off my rear. "Ready to go back now?"

He grinned. "Race ya?"

I grimaced. "Do we have to?"

It was all the answer he needed. Soon. I found myself running down a seemingly eternal path toward home behind him.

~ ~ ~

And so, our summer days passed much like our first ones together. Our conversations covered the world and reached far corners of our minds while our feet tramped through miles of Montana wilderness. A day wasted was one without Lucas, and I grew to hope more and more he felt the same.

Chapter 6

I bit my lip in concentration as my hand worked in quick short strokes across the sketchbook. A ding from my phone made my hand slip and ruin the entire sketch. "Darn it." I ripped the page out and examined it before I threw it away. *It's so peculiar how my "generic" portrait sketches end up looking like Lucas every time.* Subconsciously, my strokes seemed to turn into his strong jawline and thick dark hair whenever I picked up a pencil.

I crumpled the paper into a ball and chucked it toward the wastebasket.

"You missed." Lydia's sardonic tone broke the quiet of the room.

"I hadn't noticed." I grabbed my phone to see who the text was from. *Ugh, it's from Cora again. I'll get back to her later. I wonder when Lucas is going to respond. It's been like two hours since I texted him...*

"Emily, do you know exactly what you're getting yourself into?"

"What are you talking about?" I looked up confused as Lydia's voice broke me from my thoughts. Her clenched jaw was a clear sign she was not in a good mood.

"Lucas is a junior in high school with an unknown background. You are a freshman with zero romantic experience."

Affronted at this attack, I sat up to face her. "He's young for his class. He literally just turned sixteen in June. And I turned fifteen in June, so we're only a year apart." My voice grew colder. "I've spent way more time with him this summer than you have, so I certainly trust my own judgment more than yours. Besides, as I have told you a million times, we are just friends." *Though I wish we were more.* I tried going back to my sketch.

"It's exactly what I used to say about Finn, and look at us now," she said with a superior tone. "We've been dating for over a year and now maintain a healthy long-distance relationship."

Why does everything always work out for Lydia? "It's not hard if you spend all your time texting and calling each other like you guys do. Get a life already."

"Like you know anything about relationships."

I slammed my pencil down. "You know what Lydia? I'm not even in high school yet. Lucas and I are friends. Stop acting like you have your life together. You don't always know everything about everything." At this final statement, I picked up my pencil and began sketching again, clearly ending the conversation.

~ ~ ~

"What's your favorite color?" I asked Lucas one afternoon as our feet dangled into the ice-cold water of one of our favorite streams.

"What?"

"I asked what your favorite color was."

"No." He laughed. "I was confused because you suddenly switched from our conversation about examining hidden symbols and themes in the Harry Potter series to asking me what my favorite color was."

"So?"

He rolled his eyes. "Kind of a dramatic switch, is it not?"

"We've talked about a lot of deep stuff. We've even talked a little bit about me, but we have never talked about you. I know your opinion on the main cause of the civil war, but I don't know the little things about you."

"Like my favorite color?"

"Exactly. We've hung out almost every day for the past two weeks, and I don't know your favorite color."

"What an outrage," he commented drily.

"So... What is your favorite color?"

"Green. The color of the meadows in the spring, the shade of moss that covers the rocks in streams, the exact hue of my sister's..." He stopped suddenly.

"Your sister's—eyes?"

"Yeah." He left it there, and I didn't push.

"What else don't I know about you? Your favorite color is green. You have a sister. I know there's more." I nudged his shoulder with mine, and turned my most winning smile on him.

"I don't like talking about myself." He turned away and set his jaw.

"Okay, but I like talking about you, so let it out." I encouraged with a smile and nudge.

He sorta smiled, locked his gaze on a distant mountain, and let out a long breath. "My favorite food is blueberries. I could watch *Star Wars* on repeat for a year. I hate spiders. Sometimes I make up little songs on an old guitar my dad has, but I've never actually learned how to play. I'd rather be outside than inside, hands down. I could hike for hours, but I hate climbing trees because I fell once as a kid and hurt myself pretty badly. And I have a birthmark below my neck in the shape of a cloud." He said it quickly all in one breath.

"What kind of cloud?"

He smirked slightly. "My family always said it was a fluffy, white cloud. But it's a storm cloud."

"Two, no three more questions. Most importantly, what's your middle name?"

"Benjamin."

"*Benjamin?*" I squealed in delight.

"Oh just move on already. I know it's dorky."

"No, I love it I swear," I spluttered in between gales of laughter.

"Next question." He tried to conceal his own smile at my giddiness.

"Fine, *Lucas Benjamin,* what do you love the most?"

He paused for a long time. "Nature, but second I guess is being with people I care about the most."

"Cute." I couldn't help hoping perhaps she included me. "Final question, what are you most afraid of?"

"I already told you, it's spiders."

"Besides those. There has to be something."

He looked down and silently stared at our feet in the cold stream. "Being abandoned by the people I love, being the reason they left."

We sat quietly after that. I don't think either of us knew exactly what to say. I don't think he even knew why he said it. It took only one glance at his dark eyes for me to gently put my arms around him and hug his still frame.

After a few seconds, he shrugged off my embrace and muttered under his breath, "I shouldn't have said that. It's weird."

For the first time, Lucas almost looked like a small boy, and all I wanted to do was hug him again.

"It's not weird at all. We're friends. You're supposed to share personal things." I shivered from the chilly water.

"Easier said than done," he mumbled. He rolled back his shoulders and seemed to compose himself. "Enough about me. Let's talk about you now."

I groaned. "Do we have to?"

"What's your middle name?"

"I guess that means we have to. It's Elizabeth."

"Emily Elizabeth Lawrence. It's a pretty name."

"Thank you. I'll take all the credit for it."

"So Emily Elizabeth, who are you?"

Now it was my turn to look away. I mulled the question over in my head again and again, but I couldn't even begin to respond. "I guess the best answer I have for you is I'm still figuring it out," I whispered.

"Aren't we all?"

Yet the question weighed on my heart like so much else seemed to these days. I kicked my feet around in the water, allowing myself to be mesmerized by the different colored pebbles, which caught my eye. A slight breeze blew across the water, sending ripples as far as the nearest bend. When the sun caught them at just the right angle, they looked like tiny stars for just a moment.

He broke the quiet. "So. What's your favorite color?"

I looked up. "Blue."

"Boring."

"I prefer 'classic.'"

"Why blue?"

I looked up. "Because it's the same color as the sky. And wherever you go, wherever home is, there's always the same sky."

Chapter 7

I hummed quietly as I examined myself carefully in the mirror. *I'm really losing my tan fast from being away from the beach for so long.* I began to brush my hair, and noted with satisfaction that it had grown a lot over the last few weeks. *My eyes may be a bit too small, and my forehead a little too big, but at least I have nice hair.* My inspection of myself began to lead my thought train into other directions. *I wonder if Lucas thinks I'm pretty.* I tried without avail to shake these thoughts out of my head. *He's a guy. If he did, he would have asked me out already.*

"Where are you going?" Lydia's voice traveled sleepily from her bed.

"Outside."

"So you're meeting Lucas again today." Her tone held no question.

I sighed and paused in front of the door. "I don't know. We didn't make any plans."

"When was the last time you talked to Cora?"

To my guilty mind, her words came off accusatory. "I've been busy, okay? I've been answering her texts whenever I get the chance." *Which isn't often.* "I'll talk to her later. Right now, I'm working on making new friends instead of living in the past like some people I know." This was quickly moving in the direction of an argument.

Lydia yawned unconcernedly and sat up. "You've made one 'friend,' even if he's just that." Her long body rolled out of bed. "Just because I'm sticking with my tried and true friends, who happen to be in California, doesn't mean I'm living in the past."

"Whatever." I tried to leave, but her voice stopped me again.

"Be careful, Emily. In your quest to quickly adjust to a new place and surround yourself with new people, or rather one person, you might find the friends you leave behind are the ones who were true all along."

"I'm not leaving Cora behind."

"Well then, what do you call leaving her texts unanswered for days at a time?"

"A short leave of absence. I told you, I'll answer her later." *Every time I talk to Cora, it's like a stab in the gut, a reminder of what I'm missing. You don't understand how hard it is because you take out your grief on everyone else.*

Her laughter followed me out the door. "Whatever you say."

"And leave my phone alone," I shouted as a final retort.

Chapter 8

"What are you doing?"

I looked down from my perch in a tree. "What do you think I'm doing?" I was getting bored of sketching and had been hoping Lucas would make an appearance.

"Sitting in a tree."

I could tell he was in one of his dark moods. I sighed and climbed down a couple of branches before jumping the rest of the way down. "What do you want to do?"

"I don't know. Nothing, really."

I grabbed his hand. "Come on, let's go on a walk or something."

I set off, and he reluctantly followed.

After about a minute of my dragging him around as he stared ahead morosely, I decided enough was enough. "Let's try something different." I turned to him and grinned. "Remember you said you could run for miles without stopping? Shall we test this theory?" Without a pause, I turned and ran. I didn't have to look behind me to know he was following.

We ran through the forest without stopping. Branches whipped my hair and brambles scratched my legs. But the sound of my feet hitting the ground made me go faster and faster. I was always aware of Lucas behind me.

Finally, we reached an open meadow. The steady wind relieved my flushed face, and I paused to gasp for breath.

"Tired, huh?" He laughed.

"Well, at least you're smiling again." I managed a lopsided grin between my struggles for air.

His smile fell a little. "Yeah, but just getting your mind off something does nothing to solve the problem. At some point, you have to stop avoiding it and meet the problem head on."

I could tell he was lost in his own thoughts. His eyebrows furrowed in concentration. "Can we sit down for a second?"

He didn't wait for an answer but settled down on a log.

"What is the problem?" I couldn't contain my curiosity.

He sighed. "You don't want to hear it."

"I'm your friend. Of course, I want to hear it. Keeping the problem to yourself doesn't do much to solve it, either." I was doing my best to be helpful and be a good friend, but his eyes were rather distracting.

"No, Ems. I hate burdening people with my personal issues."

I rolled my eyes in frustration. "We've known each other for over a month now. We've both told each other lots about ourselves. You're not burdening me."

"Well, don't say I didn't warn you." He took a deep breath. "My mom died when I was really young. She was hit by a drunk driver and died instantly. It's always just been me, my dad, and my sister, Emily."

Sadness was plain in his expression, and I hurt for him. "I'm sorry."

"I don't remember her. I think I just miss having a mother in my life."

"But still—"

"Anyway, it's been hard for my dad raising us alone. Dad has always loved nature, but Mom only tolerated it because she loved him, and she knew he couldn't be happy in the city. According to my sister, she talked about us reentering the real world when we grew up and doing something big with our lives. When she died, my dad sort of became obsessive about her dream." He didn't talk for a while. "My sister, of course, was all for it. She'd been champing at the bit for years to leave this place. She got good grades, went to a good college. Now she's working her way through medical school, so she can study some brain condition some day." He clamped his jaw shut for a few seconds before taking a deep breath. "My dad is so damned proud of her, but he doesn't realize—" His voice broke. "She's never coming home."

He looked away, but not before I saw the glint of tears in his eyes. I felt helpless, sitting there quietly. I couldn't think of anything to say.

"She hasn't come back since she left for college five years ago. She always has an excuse: she's too busy, it's too expensive, it's her friend's birthday, she can't miss school. BS, all of it. She hasn't called my dad in three months, and yet he talks about her every day. Once in a while, she'll say she's coming home, but she never does. It's like a part of his heart breaks whenever it happens, but he tries to pretend he's fine." He shook his head in frustration and then stood up and began pacing. "Can you imagine? First of all, nothing I ever do could ever come close to her. She's his pride and joy. And second, I have to watch, every day, how a little part of him dies when he goes to bed without hearing from her. Day after day after day after day." His voice became angry. "It would be nice if he got mad at her for a change, but he takes it out on himself and on me."

"Do you miss her, your sister I mean?" My voice was quiet, so low I wasn't sure if he heard me at first. But my words stopped his pacing, and he stared straight ahead into the trees before finally responding. "She was my best friend, my only friend for a long time. She was always happy." His voice barely betrayed a hint of the open wound I knew rested on his heart. "I know it was hard for her. She had to be kind of a mother to both me and Dad, but she was what kept us together. God, I miss coming home and hearing her singing upstairs as loud as she could while she made the beds or cleaned." He kinda smiled. "She used to force me to sing with her sometimes while we worked together on the chores. We both have terrible voices."

Lucas continued with more eagerness in his voice. "During the tourist season, my dad worked long hours at his shop, so the two of us messed around in the woods for hours. We were obsessed with trying to catch squirrels."

I laughed. "Did you ever succeed?"

"Heck no." His laughter slowly faded. "So, now you've heard the sad sob story of Lucas Wright." He stopped his pacing and smiled wryly at me. "You must think I'm a total wuss now."

"Never." I wanted to say nothing he ever could do would make me think less of him. It didn't matter whether he was brave or not, but I couldn't find the words. *I wish I were a little more like Lydia at times like this.*

"I usually try not to think about it. It's been six years, after all. Besides, everybody has their own problems, and mine are no greater than others'. Most of the time, it's easy not to remember any of it." He let out a long breath and looked away. "But today is her birthday, and today is the day when I can't forget her as much as I'd like to." He walked a little way farther, then motioned for me to come.

I followed to where he had paused, gazing into the distance. We stood at the edge of a cliff looking out into a large valley. The sun hit his face at just the right angle, accentuating his tanned skin and angular features, the unconventional handsomeness I found so attractive. One of the things about Montana I was learning to love was the way every moment was like a Polaroid, a clear and beautiful image. I wished I could hold the way his face looked at this moment in my memory forever.

A light breeze ran through our hair. I closed my eyes, savoring the coolness and the peace it brought me. Perhaps it also gave me the courage for what I did next.

I opened my eyes. Just as the sun began to set over the hills, I leaned over and kissed his warm cheek. Then I closed my arms around him in a hug. "Thanks for telling me. I guess I'm kind of a pain in your life, too."

His body tensed at first, but then he relaxed and put his arms around me. "You're a nice kind of pain though, Ems."

I rested my head on his shoulder, and we stayed there for a long time. I savored the moment in my heart, and would keep it close for a long time.

Finally, he pulled me even closer and whispered into my hair, "The sun's starting to set. We'd better head back." Then he slowly let me go, and began to walk back, making sure I was close behind.

I reluctantly followed him home, wishing the special moment had never ended. It was then I knew the girlish fancies overpowering my mind had become something a little more than a passing crush, something I didn't even try to understand.

~ ~ ~

We parted ways when we reached the road to my house.

"See you tomorrow?" I wasn't sure of his plans.

"Yeah." His mood had brightened during our walk. He had his hands shoved in his pockets and smiled his goodbye before turning toward his home.

My heart felt full to bursting, and I could barely contain myself from singing at the top of my lungs all the way up the driveway. The aches of missing my old home, the questions weighing on my heart, the tension and fighting going on in my new home were nothing because Lucas made everything feel all right.

Chapter 9

Two weeks later, we found ourselves back at the overlook. My romantic fantasies continued, and I wondered if maybe this time he would kiss me.

"Have you ever dated anyone?" His question came out of nowhere, but my heart began to pound, and I wondered if this was going where I thought it was.

"No."

"Have you ever liked someone?"

"Well yeah, but it never went anywhere." His interrogation made me feel slightly embarrassed about my lack of a love life.

"So, you've never gone on a date?"

"Nope." I laughed shakily. "I haven't even started my freshman year of high school yet, though."

He looked mildly surprised but didn't say anything.

"Have you?"

"Yeah," he responded quietly.

I couldn't prevent the mild twinge of jealousy. "Who?"

"Well, I have a girlfriend. You probably don't know her."

All my building anticipation deflated in an instant. I turned to face the other way, so he wouldn't see the devastation in my expression. "Oh." I swallowed the lump rising in my throat. "What's her name?"

"Harper."

"Why haven't you introduced me to her yet?" My voice sounded unnaturally high, even to my own ears. *I'm not at all ready for this. I thought Lucas and I were good friends, but apparently not if he's kept this from me the whole time. And what is wrong with his girlfriend if she's fine with him hanging out with some girl he's just met? Has he been lying to both of us?*

"She's always gone in the summer. Her parents are divorced, so she stays with her mom during the summer."

I couldn't read the emotion on his face, but I could certainly feel the dark clouds of emotion in my own heart. *What kind of guy is he for leading me on this whole time, acting like my best friend, and then wheeling around and dropping the bomb he's in a relationship?*

"Do you miss her?"

"I guess." His voice sounded monotone.

I didn't dare let my hopes rise again. *Obviously, I'm not important to him if he kept this from me for so long.* "You don't sound very convinced."

"I haven't heard from her in three weeks."

"Oh. Well are you guys still dating then?"

"I think. This is the first time I've ever dated someone, so I don't know how breakups work."

"Do you want to break up with her?"

"I don't know."

I didn't ask him any questions for a while, mostly because he didn't seem to want to answer. Finally, I broke the silence. "She must be really pretty." My voice was wistful.

"Yeah." His expression broke into a half-smile for the first time. "She's really tall and has pale, ivory skin. And violet eyes, big violet eyes."

I regarded my own short, tanned legs. "So basically, the opposite of me?"

"I guess."

The silence between us felt awkward for the first time. *So, I'm clearly not his type.* I knew asking more questions would only make the pain creeping through my entire being worse, but I couldn't resist one more. "Have you ever kissed her?"

"Of course. We dated for like four or five months."

A pained breath escaped my lips. I searched the empty air for an excuse to escape. "My mom said I have to be back for dinner." I jumped up too quickly.

He looked at me curiously. "Are you okay?"

"Yeah, I just have a bit of a headache."

"Well, give me a sec, and I'll walk you home."

"No. Don't bother." I tossed my response over my shoulder. "It's quicker if I go alone."

"It's your choice." He was starting to get up and brush himself off.

"Bye then." I didn't wait for a reply before I began jogging away. As soon as I was out of sight in the trees, I took off at a sprint. My toes barely touched the ground as my hair flew behind me. The wind was blowing against my face, making me shiver. Tears streamed down my cheeks and were left far behind me as I raced the oncoming night.

I paused before entering the house to brush off stray tears and rub my eyes and nose. I took a deep breath, opened the door, and quickly escaped up the stairs. As soon as I was in my room, I shut the door firmly behind me and leaned against it with my eyes closed. I caught my breath, opened my eyes, and noticed my sister on the bed in the corner.

"Lydia?"

Sobs racked her entire body, and the light from her computer lit up her red, watery eyes.

"I've never seen you cry over a movie before. Is it some tear jerker or something?"

When she heard my voice, her hands shook as she removed her earbuds. "Hey, Em," she replied in a small voice. "It's a comedy, actually."

"What?"

She interrupted me before I could finish. "Finn and I broke up."

"Aw, sis." I watch her face crumple again, trying to hold back more tears. "Gosh, this has been a bad night for both of us."

"What do you mean?" She let out a croaky laugh. "You've been with Lucas, basically your boyfriend, all afternoon."

"No." I tried to control my voice, but it cracked anyway. "He has a girlfriend, actually."

"What the hell?" Her sobbing turned into hysterical laughter.

"It's not funny." Now I was crying, too.

"Don't you find it ironic? We move to this miserable place. My boyfriend of eighteen months breaks up with me after only two months of a long-distance relationship. Meanwhile, your first major crush has been leading you on this whole time and then announces he's already in a relationship. What a crappy night this is." Her laughter turned into gut-wrenching sobs again. "But what the hell, at least we're blooming, right, Mom?"

Her pain was raw and gaping. I couldn't help but let my own tears subside as I went over and climbed into her bed. Usually my sister was the one to hold me, but this time I put my arms around her. Her head fell onto my shoulder.

"Ouch." I rubbed the spot where her head had hit my collarbone. "And now, I'll be taking a trip to the emergency room because you almost killed me. Actually, is there even a hospital in Montana?"

"You're not even funny." She moaned between sobs.

I rested my head against hers and considered how our roles had switched in one night, even as my own tears fell on her head.

We stayed curled up next to each other with our hair and tears tangled together for a long time. Mine finally subsided, but Lydia's sobs still silently shook her body. It was a miracle our mother hadn't heard us, but the banging of the pans as she made dinner drowned out the sound.

"Girls, come down to eat," she called from the dining room.

We exchanged horrified glances at the state we were in. Her eyes pleaded with me to do something. I cleared my throat. "Uh, Lydia and I already ate. We're not hungry."

We remained still in the silence which followed.

"Are you sure? I don't remember seeing either of you down here." I could barely hear her voice through the thick, wooden walls.

"We, uh, we ate a lot of food outside, like midafternoon. So, we're still stuffed."

"Okay."

The disappointment in her voice was clear, but she didn't insist we come down. And she didn't come up.

My sister's body relaxed again, and this time she was still.

My loud, outgoing sister felt small as she lay nestled against me. Black streaks trailed below her closed eyes. "I miss California." Her voice was even smaller. "I miss my friends. I miss going to the beach. I miss going to school and knowing everyone." Her tone released a tidal wave of grief, long suppressed in my own heart.

She could barely choke out the words, and her voice cracked with almost every syllable. She took a shaky breath. "I miss the train three miles away from home. It woke me up at night every time it blew the horn. I miss the sunshine, and wearing big coats on the three days a year it rained." It chilled my whole being to hear her speaking like this. I had never seen Lydia devoid of strength, emotionally and physically, with anguish in her eyes instead of anger to reflect the pain she'd been in for months.

She laughed and wiped away tears at the same time. "I miss morning runs with my cross country team, and how it only took five minutes to drive to everyone's house. I miss Finn picking us up for school in the morning. I miss how he used to surprise me in the hallways and hug me so tightly I could barely breathe." Her sobs rose in intensity. "I miss being mad at him. Then he'd say sorry with his big blue eyes, and I had to forgive him. I miss pretending to be surprised when he asked me to all the school dances the same way every time. I miss going on double dates with Cade and Lou. I miss Lou so much. And God knows, I miss Finn." She buried her head in her pillow, struggling to quell the whimpers. Finally, she whispered into the darkness of our room, "I miss him more than I even know how to say."

I hugged her for a while, but my eyes strayed outside to the moon. I knew Lucas was staring at it, too. He told me once he stared at it at night as he falls asleep. Somehow knowing he was looking at the same thing I was brought him closer to my aching heart.

I snapped myself out of it. *Lucas has a girlfriend. Get over this.* I pulled my eyes away from the sky. "Lydia?"

"Yeah?" She responded groggily.

"Why did he...I mean what did he say when he..."

She sighed. "He told me he loved me. He said he loved me more than any girl he had ever known. But it wasn't the same being far away, and our relationship was too painful this way. He thinks it'll be easier and less demanding for both of us or something." She stopped for a minute, probably swallowing back tears. "Em, here's the thing. Guys are idiots. They'll tell you exactly what you want to hear, and then the next thing you know, they're gone and have moved on. If a guy's emotions are the size of a blueberry, our emotions are bigger than a pumpkin or a watermelon or some other large fruit."

"That was the worst analogy I have ever heard." I giggled.

"Shut up. I was trying to be an inspirational and helpful older sister."

"You just had like an hour-long breakdown."

"God, you're so annoying. No wonder Lucas hasn't broken up with his girlfriend for you."

"Ouch."

"Too soon, huh? I'm sorry, I shouldn't have said it."

"No. You're right, though. I'm just a lowly, lovesick, annoying freshman. And he's sixteen with a gorgeous girlfriend. No one would pick me over her."

"Hey, don't be so hard on yourself. This is, like, your first actual crush. Things will work out for you someday if not now, I promise."

"How comforting. So, now I'm gonna find true love when I'm forty."

"You know it's not what I meant."

I was angry and emotionally spent. "I'm going to bed."

"Emily." Her voice sounded remorseful. "Don't be mad. Please. I was just trying to help."

"I know. I'm not mad at you." I rolled over and closed my eyes, willing myself to go to sleep. But all I could see was Lucas's smiling face in my dreams. It just made the pain worse, knowing I would always just be like a little sister to him. A small voice in my head whispered I was being over-dramatic about the whole situation. But sometimes it was nice just to dwell in my own misery.

Chapter 10

The next day, I refused to get out of bed and instead, wallowed for hours. I tossed and turned and eventually threw off all the covers, sleeping and staring blankly into space in turn.

Lydia had left early to take my brother on a hike, and my parents had gone to the nearby town of Bozeman, so I was alone in the house.

Finally, I dragged myself to a sitting position. My head spun and ached from the emotion and exhaustion of crying and lying down for hours. I let my chin rest on the windowsill and stared morosely at the sky. It was hot, and there was a noticeable lack of a breeze to brighten my day.

A rock cracking against the glass broke through my depressed thoughts. I angrily threw the window open only to stare down at a familiar face. "What the hell, Lucas? You could've broken my window."

A cheery voice responded, "Someone woke up cranky today. Come down, sleepyhead. Get dressed 'cause I have an adventure planned."

It was the last thing I wanted to do. But with no other options and no excuses not to go, it seemed the only thing I was going to do.

"I'm coming." I sighed and slammed the window shut.

For the first time, I didn't care how I looked as I stomped out the door toward Lucas. I hadn't brushed my hair or washed my face, much less put on decent clothes.

"Well, aren't you a bright ray of sunshine."

"You aren't exactly on my favorite persons list, either."

"Well, you're number one on mine." He grinned.

So funny considering you were mine until you completely destroyed me yesterday. "If you are trying to cheer me up, you are failing miserably."

"Considering you haven't killed me yet, I think I'm doing an excellent job." He walked on quickly through the woods.

"Where are we going? Any mountain lions or bears nearby? Maybe you'll get eaten."

"Sheesh, you are in a bad mood."

I sullenly stared ahead at the ground.

"What's the matter?"

You. "I'm fine."

"That's the biggest lie I've ever heard."

"What do you want me to say?" I turned away angrily, slightly enjoying how uncomfortable I was making him.

"Did I say something yesterday?"

"It doesn't matter."

"Oh God. What did I do?"

"I said it doesn't matter. Just shut up, will you?" My voice was steadily rising in pitch.

He didn't respond for a while.

Somehow releasing all this anger made me feel worse.

"Please, if I did something wrong, tell me. You're my friend. I don't want you to be mad at me."

I didn't reply, knowing I would say something I'd regret.

He sighed. "Well, I have something to tell you."

"What?" I frowned.

"I called Harper last night because I was thinking a lot about what we talked about yesterday. And now we're not together anymore."

Trust the Wind

"I didn't tell you to break up with her yesterday." *This just gets weirder and weirder.*

"No, no I didn't break up with her." He stopped, and then he seemed to struggle to explain himself. "It was mutual, I guess you could say."

"Well that's the best way to end things." I paused and muttered under my breath, "Not as if I would know."

"It's been too long since we talked, and apparently she met someone else." He added the last part quickly with a glum tone.

I didn't respond, not daring to give way to the hope blooming in my chest.

He didn't seem bothered by my silence. "You can't imagine how nice it feels to be so free and unattached again."

"Actually, I can imagine. It's not so great after you get more used to it," I muttered, mostly to myself.

He turned to look at me with a grin and began to laugh. "Gosh, you are negative today. But you're adorable, even when you're mad."

I cringed at the word. "Adorable? Gee thanks."

He laughed harder. "Well, what do you want me to call you? Drop-dead gorgeous? That would be weird."

I could feel my face heating with anger. "And why would it be weird?"

"Because you're my friend. You don't go around telling your friends how beautiful they are. You just sort of expect them to know, I guess." He chuckled. "It's their boyfriends' or girlfriends' job to do it." *Ouch. The obvious friendzone.* "Well, I guess single people like me only get their friends calling them adorable. It's very comforting."

"Don't be ridiculous. You already know you're pretty and all."

He seemed unperturbed by his words as he strolled through the trees.

I didn't respond, and merely allowed his words to soak in as they simultaneously pricked my heart and healed it. By now, the silence between us felt more comfortable. Whatever tension had filled the air moments before had dissipated, leaving behind the friendly quiet we were used to. I kept my eyes on his feet, letting him lead me wherever it was we were going. I noticed the leaves, which crackled and gave way under his steps. Their unique coloring mesmerized me.

"Fall is almost here," Lucas quietly noted.

"Well, now since we're being philosophical, have you ever noticed how leaves are a little like snowflakes?"

His nose wrinkled. "In what way?"

"No snowflake is like another, just like the coloring of each of the leaves in fall is always slightly different."

"Yeah, I guess. I never really thought about it."

My thoughts tumbled on. "Every season kind of has its own version of a snowflake. Fall has leaves. Spring has unique newborn plants and animals. And summer..."

"Clouds," he finished for me. "Summer has clouds. Each one has its own shape and appearance."

"You're right. Summer does have incredible clouds, like the light fluffy ones, which look like dinosaurs dancing in the sky."

"Dinosaurs dancing in the sky?"

"I don't know. It was just the first thing that popped into my mind."

"Well, you know dark clouds are unique, too."

"Not really. They always have the same dark and depressing look."

"You really can be such a typical California girl sometimes." He grumbled. "Calling dark clouds depressing."

"Dark clouds mean rain, and everyone knows you can't do anything in the rain." I couldn't help but laugh when I said it, knowing he would freak out.

"Oh, my gosh. I love the rain. There's lots to do in the rain. Haven't you ever gone running during spring showers and gotten so soaked you were freezing cold? And then ran back inside and taken a super-hot shower and watched as the bathroom windows steamed up from the hot inside but cold outside? You've never just sat by the window with a blanket for hours and watched as the raindrops raced down the pane?"

"I love the game. I used to make bets with my brother while we were in the car for which one would win."

"See? You do like the rain. You just haven't embraced it."

"I don't think I've ever met an outdoorsy boy who likes the rain."

"Well I'm not like a lot of boys."

I smiled. "That's definitely true."

"We made it."

We stopped in front of a tiny creek.

"This is it? I've come to expect a lot more from our adventures."

He pretended to be horrified. "Is this it? Yes, it most certainly is. This small river—"

"Creek." I corrected him. "It's not a river."

"This *creek* is the one and only Emily Creek."

"I'm so honored. You named a tiny stream after me."

"Actually, it was named after my sister." The silence was palpable for an instant, as the thought of her seemed to sober him for a minute.

"Ouch."

"But it can include you now, too, I guess."

"How generous of you." I admit it sounded snide.

"It's what good friends are for." The words rolled off his tongue easily. He hadn't a care in the world as he unknowingly tossed my emotions around like a washing machine.

"Good friends, huh?" Something inside my chest ached.

"I met you...almost exactly two months ago. It's crazy. Feels like it's been much longer."

Two months ago, I thought we would be more than friends by this point. "And yet it doesn't. The days run together, but at the same time, they don't."

"Hmm. Interesting way of putting it."

I was content to watch him skip pebbles for a while.

"Do you miss them still?"

"Miss who?" My mind still wandered in the clouds.

"Your friends back home."

The guilt of his words jarred me awake. "Um, I guess." I tried to keep my voice casual and carefree, hiding the emotional shock and emptiness they drew from inside me.

"You never talk about them."

"There's Eloise, and Natalie, and Jake, and Liz, and...Cora." I choked slightly on the last name. *Shoot. I forgot to text her back. I'll just do it when I get home.*

"Who's Cora?"

He had to go and pick her to talk about. "She's just a girl I was friends with back in California." It was like she could hear me, even from thousands of miles away. Guilt flooded through my being like the stream at my feet ran through my toes.

"What's she like?" His tone was mildly curious, but his eyes never strayed from the pebbles he threw or the water he tossed them into.

I took a deep breath. "Um. Well, she loves the beach. She likes to walk along the shore or sit and tan on a towel, but she hates going under big waves. She thinks it's hilarious to turn on the windshield wipers of the car even on perfectly clear days. She listens to Broadway music all the time, especially with Lydia. She loves reading old books, like not just published a long time ago, but books whose covers are practically falling off. And she absolutely *adores* chocolate bars. The two of us loved to go to her grandpa's house and swim or talk to him for hours." I stopped myself, surprised I had said so much.

"She sounds like a really good friend."

"Yes," I whispered. "Yes, she is." *And clearly I'm a terrible one for not responding to her in days.*

"You don't talk about California very much."

"Yeah, I guess not. But I'm here now. Seems stupid to me to live in the past. Besides, I have new friends like you now." I yawned and rested my head on my hand.

He seemed to notice my exhaustion from the night before. "You look tired. We should probably head back."

I wordlessly got up and followed him back down the path.

"You know, I'm glad you moved here." Lucas slowed his pace to fall in step next to me and put his arm around my shoulders.

"Now this is just awkward." His brotherly affection was painful, as much as it warmed me inside.

He laughed. "Nobody ever said good friendship wasn't awkward sometimes."

I leaned my head against him, wishing his heart felt the same things as mine. "You think we'll always be good pals?"

"It depends."

"On what?"

"You."

"What do you mean?"

"You can't be too popular for me."

"Me? Popular? Those two things couldn't be more opposite."

"And one more thing."

"What?"

"You can't fall in love with me."

My head jerked up, wondering if he'd figured out my secret. "What?" My heart pounded, but the innocent expression on his face relieved me slightly.

"I know I'm pretty cute but I'm taken."

I laughed and shoved him away from me. "Yeah, by a squirrel?"

He scowled at me. "I'm taken by myself."

"There's a new one, falling in love with yourself. Just a tad self-absorbed, Lucas?"

"I'm just saying we're both happily single, and I don't want you to ruin our friendship by falling in love with me." He grinned impishly.

"Oh sure. Well, what if you fall in love with me first? I'm pretty drop-dead gorgeous."

"You are pretty hot."

I appraised his expression to see if he was being serious. "As hot as Mount Everest in the winter."

"Ha ha. Very funny, Luke."

"There's a new one."

"I actually like the nickname. I'm going to keep it for you."

We arrived back at the split in the road. One way led to my house, and one led to his.

"Bye. I'm glad you're not cranky anymore."

"Bye, Luke." I laughed as I said it and waved farewell as I walked on alone. As the grass crunched beneath my feet, I looked up at the sky. The clouds swayed to the invisible music of the wind. *You know, if nature was alive, I think the wind and the clouds would be good friends. Because without the clouds, you could never see the wind or know it was there. And the cloud, in order for it to go where it needs to go, always has to trust the wind.*

Chapter 11

I walked into the house with a smile on my face. My mother sat on the couch reading a book. The lamplight softened the small wrinkles on her forehead and around her eyes from the years of stress of being a mom and her career. Her dark brown hair was swept back in a soft ponytail, with lingering strands framing her face. She looked beautiful, even with little makeup on. She looked up, as if she sensed my gaze on her. Her wise green eyes appraised me, and I knew they missed nothing.

"Come, sit down with me. I feel like I never see you these days." She set down her book and rearranged the blanket on her lap.

I was slightly wary, knowing my mother always had a purpose whenever she invited me so clearly to a conversation. "Let me go change into more comfortable clothes, and then I'll come down."

I changed quickly but made my way back down the stairs slowly, trying to go through all possible topics she might bring up.

I finally sat down warily in the armchair across from her. "So, where is everybody?"

"Dad took Lydia and Liam to see a movie."

"What?" I protested. "Why didn't they wait for me?"

She looked awkward for a moment. "Lydia and I got into an argument again, and Dad decided it was a good time to get her and Liam out of the house. Lydia and I have been together alone a lot with her doing college applications and whatever else it is that she does on her computer. Maybe we both needed a break." She took a breath and resettled herself. "Besides, the movie started thirty minutes ago. It's almost seven o'clock, Emmy."

"Oh, my gosh. I didn't realize it was so late."

"Mhhm." She sipped something from a mug, probably tea. "How's Cora?"

"Fine, I think."

"You think?"

"We haven't talked much recently." *I responded yesterday, but before then, I hadn't talked to her in a week.*

Lines appeared between her eyebrows, but she didn't comment. A long silence followed.

"You've been hanging out a lot with Lucas recently."

It's finally out. The real reason for this conversation. "Mom," I began, "it's not what you think."

"What do you mean?" She inquired innocently.

I gave her a look. "You know what I mean. Lucas and I are just friends, Mom."

"Honey, it's fine if you two like each other. It's not a problem."

I interrupted her right there. "Mom. We don't like each other, okay? Lucas broke up with his girlfriend just this morning. We are just good friends. And *only* good friends."

She raised her eyebrows. "Lucas had a girlfriend?"

I didn't respond.

"Well anyway, I'm glad you two are such good friends." The conversation stopped awkwardly.

"He's been so nice showing you around. And you'll know someone when you start high school." She took another long sip.

This is tortuous.

"So what is it that you do in the woods all day?"

I turned red. "Mom. We just go on long hikes, and sometimes we walk to town and stuff. It's not a big deal."

She got a mischievous glint in her eye. "That's a lot of time in the woods talking and hiking. Has he kissed you?"

"Mom." I was horrified. "Of course not. I just finished explaining to you. We are just good friends."

"I know, I know. Just making sure. You know you can always tell me when you like someone. It's okay if you like him, and he doesn't like you back."

"Oh my gosh, Mom." I cringed inwardly. "I'm going upstairs."

"No, we're having a conversation. Stay down here."

I fell back into my seat reluctantly.

"Lydia always tells me if she likes anyone."

"Okay, that's it. I'm out."

"Emily, Lucas is cute and really nice. It's normal for you to like him."

"Mother, how many times do I have to tell you? Lucas and I are *just friends*." I started to walk out of the room.

"Emily, come back," she pleaded. "I'll stop talking about this. I promise."

"Goodnight, Mom."

"You didn't even eat dinner."

"I ate a late lunch." I let out a deep breath, but my cheeks were flushed with embarrassment.

When I reached my room, I flopped onto my bed and grabbed my phone. There was only one new message, and it was from Lucas.

can u tell me why u were mad at me when i see u next

I considered what to respond.

maybe
maybe

He responded quickly.

wanna go see a movie tomorrow?

sure

I couldn't contain the slight fluttering in my stomach as I fell asleep.

Chapter 12

"What are you grinning about?" I looked curiously at Lydia.

She glanced up from her computer screen, her face lit up from its brightness, and she flashed a rare smile. "I finished my NYU essays, and they are...well I think they're the best essays I've written."

"NYU essays?" I asked uncertainly.

"New York University? I thought I told you that I was applying there. It's my first choice, for God's sake."

I broke eye contact from her steady scrutiny. My gaze drifted out the window to the bird's nest perched in the eaves of our extended porch roof. "Mrs. Bennett's eggs hatched."

Lydia snorted. "Where've you been? They haven't just hatched, they did it weeks ago. They flew away already and are probably long gone."

It was quiet again for a while, but I could feel her eyes searching me. "You've grown up a lot this summer."

"I have? How?" I turned back to face her.

She nodded with an unreadable smile on her lips. "You're just...older somehow. Your face has matured a lot. It's funny. You remind me of those old pictures of Grandma."

My heart ached familiarly, and I could tell Lydia missed Grandma, too. "You think she's doing okay by herself in California?"

Lydia forced a smile and a laugh. "I'm sure she is. After all, Jordan and Alex are still there."

We both grimaced at the thought of our weird older cousins. "Poor Grandma."

It became quiet again, both of us lost in our own thoughts.

"NYU, huh? It's awfully far away." I tried to sound casual.

"It's only four years. And I still have to get in, after all. Besides, I don't leave for college for another twelve months."

"A year isn't long," I replied with a hint of sadness I couldn't control.

She laughed. "It is in Montana. There is *nothing* to do here."

I laughed with her. "Speak for yourself. I have a movie to get ready for."

She rolled her eyes as I stood up to leave. "Bye then, Miss Popular."

"Oh, shut up."

Chapter 13

From my bedroom window, I saw Lucas pull up in his truck. I grabbed my phone and wallet and hurried down the stairs.

"Bye, Mom. I'll be back later."

"Wait. Where are you going?"

Her voice stopped me as I rushed out the door. "I'm going to a movie. I told you already."

She gave me a knowing look. "Okay. You have been spending an awful lot of time with Lucas in the woods, and now at the movies. Just remember I trust you. Don't do anything to break it."

I sighed and threw up my hands in exasperation. "Mom."

"I'm just saying." She walked back into the kitchen.

I rolled my eyes, shut the door behind me a little harder than necessary, and ran out to his truck.

Honk honk. I almost dropped my phone in surprise. "What the heck, Lucas?" I glared at him as I continued walking around to the other side of the vehicle.

"Hurry up and get in."

"Isn't this illegal? Aren't you not allowed to drive anyone until after you've had your license for a year?"

"Who made you a cop?"

He shut me up for the time being, but I had no problem losing myself in my thoughts. *New York is a long way away from Montana. I can't believe Lydia wants to go so far from us.*

I must have looked nervous because Lucas glanced over. "Are you okay? You've gone into Bozeman before."

"I dunno. I'm just thinking. Lydia wants to go to college in New York."

He didn't say anything for a while. "Well, I invited some of my friends to meet you."

Distraction. Nice one, Lucas. "You did?" My excitement faded a bit.

"Yeah. You don't mind, right? I haven't seen any of them all summer."

"No, I don't mind. So it's gonna be me and a bunch of junior guys?"

"No, it's only a couple of people. Besides, they invited Lucy, too."

"Who's Lucy?"

"Jack's girlfriend. She's nice. You'll like her. Oh, and Jack's little brother, Matt, is coming, and he's a sophomore."

"Okay." My nerves were suddenly heightened at the prospect of meeting so many new people.

We didn't speak until we pulled into the parking lot in front of the movie theater. "Well, here we are." Lucas sounded awkward.

"No, duh." My gaze paused on the group of teenagers standing in front of the old building. The three boys were laughing at what I assumed was some immature joke, while only a small smile danced at the girl's lips as her eyes glanced away. At the sight of his truck, they all began to approach as we got out of the car.

"Well, well, well. If it isn't Lucas and his freshie girlfriend."

Immediately, I felt my face begin to flush.

Out of the corner of my eye, I saw the girl's face dart over to the boy who had just spoken and give him look.

He turned red and shuffled his feet awkwardly. "Just joking, friends." He tried to laugh it off.

The girl walked up to me and gave me a hug. Her friendly smile reached her large brown eyes. "Just ignore him, Emily. I'm Lucy. Nice to meet you."

"Nice to meet you, too." My voice sounded soft, concealing my nerves. I could barely meet her confident gaze.

"Ooh, getting some heat from your girlfriend, Jack?" One of the other kids snickered.

"Aw shut up, Ben. Lucy here loves me." He threw his arm around her slender shoulder and kissed her head.

"Save it." She pushed him away, but couldn't hide the smile on her face.

"Since your boy, who is a 'friend,' isn't introducing us—" he gave Lucas a pointed look. "I will introduce myself. I'm Jack. Nice to meet you. This is Ben, and that's Matt."

Ben grinned, but Matt only smiled shyly.

I couldn't help but smile.

"So, you guys aren't dating?" Matt inquired politely.

"No, we are not." Lucas spoke for the first time. He seemed more subdued than usual.

He didn't have to say it so quickly.

Matt looked surprised, but I didn't miss how his eyes flickered as he eyed me up and down.

I met his eyes with a level stare as I felt my cheeks redden with discomfort, making sure he knew I had noticed. He flushed and looked the other way.

"Well, are we gonna see the movie or not?" Jack broke the silence and began walking toward the ticket booth. He looked mildly surprised when Lucy headed toward me instead of following behind him.

She linked her elbow with mine like we were old friends, and leaned down to whisper in my ear, "Don't worry about Luke. He'll come around."

My eyes widened. "How did you know?"

She laughed, a light tinkling sound. "It's not hard to tell. He gets in these moods sometimes. You'll get used to it."

"He doesn't like me, so it doesn't really matter."

"Oh, really? Give it some time."

"Lucy," Jack called. "Hurry up."

"Oh shoot. I didn't get a ticket." I reached into my pocket to grab money when Lucas materialized next to me.

"I got one for you."

"Oh. Thanks." I smiled up at him.

Jack had grabbed Lucy's hand, but she turned around and winked at me before he pulled her inside.

Luke looked down questioningly as we followed them in. "What was that about?"

"Nothing." My quick response and telltale blush didn't seem to faze him.

Chapter 14

We walked out of the theater laughing about the cheesiness of the movie we'd just seen. Ben and Jack mimicked the awkward romance of the two main characters while the rest of us held our stomachs with uncontrollable mirth. As we headed toward the cars, Matt came up beside me.

"Hey, let me give you my number."

"Oh." I looked up in surprise. "Uh, yeah sure." I handed him my phone, and he typed in his contact info.

Lucas looked over with a curious expression.

Matt handed the phone back. "Uh, let me know if you need anything or have any questions before school starts."

I smiled my appreciation, and he looked slightly cockier as he walked away with Ben.

I turned, and Lucy hugged me goodbye. "Luke will give you my number if you need anything. It was fun talking to you." She smiled in her quiet way.

"Bye, Em." Jack casually threw out the nickname. Then, he grabbed Lucy's hand and led her away.

She waved goodbye, and I watched for a minute as the two of them walked down the small main street together. Jack was clowning around, and I could hear Lucy's giggles even from a distance.

"Are you coming or not?" Lucas waited in the front seat with his door open.

"Oh yeah. Sorry, I'm coming." I quickly opened the other door to get into the passenger seat.

He started up the old truck. "So, how do you like my friends?"

"They were all funny and nice, especially Lucy. She's so sweet."

"I knew you'd like her."

"She and Jack are adorable together."

"Yeah, they've been dating since the beginning of freshman year."

Our conversation paused awkwardly for a minute.

"Matt seemed into you."

I looked out the window. "You think?"

"Yeah. Do you like him?"

"He's nice, but—I don't know. We just met. He's not really my type."

"He's a good guy."

I interrupted him before he could continue. "I'm sure he is, but I'm not interested"

He raised his eyebrows. "Oh. So, you like someone else?"

My whole body tensed. "No."

He laughed. "Somehow, I don't believe you. Is it Jack? Because he's taken. And I'm sorry, but both Ben and Jack are meatheads."

"First of all, it's mean to call your friends names. Secondly, I said I don't like anyone." My tone clearly signaled the end of the conversation. The air was tense, so I tried distracting myself by looking out the window.

"Emily, is everything okay?" He stopped and seemed to struggle with words. "You've just been—acting weird recently."

"What do you mean?" My heart thumped so loud Luke must have been deaf not to hear it.

"I don't know. I can't put my finger on it. I feel like I know you so well, but then I remember we only met a few months ago."

"Few months can be long enough." My gut knew what was coming, and I wanted him, more than anything, to say nothing at all. Hearing it in words would make it all the more real.

"It's true." He paused.

Don't say it. Don't say it. Don't say it.

"I like being good friends with you. I don't want anything to ruin it. So, if there's anything wrong, please tell me."

Focus on the trees. You knew he thought of you only as a good friend. It's fine. Everything is fine. This is how it's always been. Take a deep breath. "No. I'm all right."

"Okay. But like even now, for example, you're acting weird."

Something inside started cracking. "What do you mean I'm acting weird? How am I acting weird? You keep telling me I am, but you won't give me any examples." My rising voice betrayed my emotion.

"Like this. Just now. You're all—emotional. I didn't say anything, and all of a sudden you're snapping at me."

"I am not snapping."

"Oh my God, Emily. Just tell me what the problem is." His hands were clenching the wheel.

You are a problem. You play with my feelings. You kind of flirt and act jealous, and then you completely friendzone me. School is a problem. My family is a problem. Stupid Montana is a problem. My life is one big massive problem. "There is no problem. Everything is *fine.*"

"You're freaking yelling at me right now. Obviously something is wrong." His jaw clenched as he tried to keep his anger down.

"Now who's the one yelling?"

"God, you can be so *annoying* sometimes."

I sucked in a small breath, and this time I really had to fight the tears.

"Emily." He sighed. "I didn't mean it like that. You were angry. I was angry, so I said something I didn't mean. Please don't take it personally."

I refused to respond. *How do I not take it personally?* We were nearing my house, and tears threatened to fall at any minute. I got ready to jump out of the car as soon as it slowed to a stop. "Well, school starts in a few days. I guess I'll see you then."

"No, Emily, stop."

"What?" My voice sounded harsh to my own ears as I continued to get out of the truck.

He grabbed my hand, stopping me in my tracks. "I'm sorry. I was trying to be a good friend." He flushed and looked me in the eye. "I...I care about you. If something is wrong I can help you with, I want to know."

I tried to smile back, but utterly failed. All I remember as I quietly slid out the door were the tears blurring my vision and the look in his eyes. An untrained eye would find them unreadable in their smoky green depths, but mine noticed a small glimmer of something new: confusion.

My steps quickened as I walked up the sloping pathway to our door. A window unrolled behind me.

"Emily."

I stopped but didn't turn around.

"Are you sure you're okay?"

I was still except for my eyelids blinking back tears. I took a deep breath. "I'm fine."

Neither of us spoke. A chill breeze rippled the ends of my hair.

"Well, bye I guess. I'll see you later." He started up the truck.

"Bye, Luke."

I didn't move again until I heard the telltale sound of crunching gravel signifying he had left. The tears fell too furiously to attempt to wipe them away. In one brief, perfectly horrible moment, the air was absolutely still. The wind completely left me.

Chapter 15

I woke up bleary-eyed to see my mom's face leaning over me with a smile and the dreaded words, "Wake up, Emily. It's time to get ready for your first day of school."

Immediately, adrenaline began to course through my bloodstream. I rolled out of bed and walked toward the bathroom, but the door wouldn't open. "Lydia."

"I'm almost done," came the cheery response.

"Morning people," I muttered sullenly.

"I heard you."

The sound of the lock being played with simply annoyed me. Finally, the door slowly opened. Lydia leaned over the sink with a makeup brush in hand, finishing up the final touches. She turned and rubbed the gloss on her lips together. "Is this too much or too little?"

"I think you're fine. It's not too much or too little." I yawned.

"Are you just saying it so I'll leave the bathroom?"

"I'm saying it because it looks fine. Now leave. It's my turn." I pushed her out the door and closed it firmly behind her.

"Sheesh. Someone woke up on the wrong side of the bed."

I examined myself carefully in the mirror, turning my head at different angles before finally grabbing the cloth to wash my face. It took me less than ten minutes to finish up in the bathroom and get dressed. Lydia came back into our room just as I walked out.

She took one look at me before she grabbed my elbow. "Oh no you don't."

"What?" I protested.

She led me into the bathroom. "This is your first day of high school, and though we may be in some stupid small town in some random part of Montana, which I don't even remember the name of, this day is a big deal." She flourished a mascara tube. "So, you are going to look the part."

"Aw, Lydia." I scowled. "It's just school."

"Just for the first week, you have to promise me. First impressions are a big deal. Remember, these kids have been going to school together for a long time. You're an outsider."

A familiar twitching feeling in my stomach resurfaced. "Aren't you nervous?"

She gently held my face still as she applied the brush across my lashes. "Yes and no. I've already been a freshman and suffered high school for three years. It's nothing exciting for me anymore. All my friends are in California. At this point, getting good grades to get into college so I can get a job back home is the only way to get me back to them. It's all that matters." She took a deep breath. "Besides, it's Montana. How hard can it be to fit in anyway?"

Chapter 16

The sheer number of people surprised me. Masses of kids of so many different appearances rushed screaming and laughing through the hallways. A big kid rudely shoved me into the lockers as he passed by and knocked the breath out of me.

Suddenly, Luke appeared at my side. "Hello."

"How did you find me?" My heart began to pound in nervousness remembering what had happened the last time we'd hung out.

"It was easy. I looked for the short, tan, blonde one." He smiled at me a smile that always seemed meant just for me. "I can always find you."

Relief flooded through me as we approached the tables for incoming freshman. *This high school thing is crazy, but no matter what, I have Lucas.*

After I told her my name, an older lady handed me a file. "Sweetie, do you need any help finding your classes?"

"No, I'll help her." Luke smiled charmingly in a manner only he could pull off.

The lady beamed. "How sweet of you."

We walked in silence, partially because it would have been difficult to hear each other over the ruckus, and partially because neither of us knew what to say.

"Well, here we are." He seemed unsure of what to do, but finally pulled me into a hug. It wasn't one of those awkward   touch-the-other-person-as-little-as-possible-then-go hugs. It was a real hug, a melt-in-his-arms one, which made me never want to go. I closed my eyes and took a shaky breath.

He hugged me tighter for a brief moment and whispered into my hair, "You'll be just fine."

My eyes began to water because I was about to be truly alone for the first time in high school. "I know." I blinked back the tears before Luke let me go. *Get yourself together, Emily. It's just high school.* "Bye." I watched his tousled hair disappear into the crowd before I turned to walk into the classroom.

Everyone stopped their conversations to look me over. I cast my eyes down and found a seat in the back.

"Hi, I'm Jacob. You don't look like you're from around here."

I turned quickly, wondering if someone could possibly be talking to me. "Oh, I'm Emily. And yeah, I just moved here from California."

"Wow, interesting. We don't meet people from there too often here." A smile broke his serious expression, and he adjusted his glasses.

"Yeah..."

The girl sitting in front of Jacob turned around. "You're from California?"

"Yup." *This is going to get old fast.*

"I'm Miranda. It's nice to meet you." She grinned, but somehow it didn't reach her eyes.

"I'm Emily. It's nice to meet you, too." *Except not really.*

"Do you play any sports?" Miranda refused to meet Jacob's eyes. Jacob himself was looking more and more uncomfortable by the minute.

"Just soccer..."

I was cut off by the teacher's greeting and request for quiet.

~ ~ ~

The day continued rather uneventfully. I met two or three people in my next class, but Jacob was the only one who seemed to take an interest in talking to me. He approached me again during passing period after the second class of the day.

"Oh. Hi again." I tried to smile and not look weirded out. *How the heck did he find me?*

He must have read my mind because he blushed slightly. "My second period was right next to yours, so I saw you when I walked out. I figured you might need some help finding your next class."

Aw, he's kinda thoughtful. "Um yeah, actually. I would really appreciate it. But aren't you a freshman, too?"

"Yeah." He fell in step next to me as we continued through the crowded halls. "But the middle school is right next to the high school, so sometimes classes overlap. By the time you get to high school, you know the buildings pretty well."

"How convenient." I had absolutely no idea what else to say.

"So, you're from California?"

He already knows. God, this is so awkward.

"Mhhm. I moved here this summer."

"Way cool. Do you miss it and all your friends and everything?"

What kind of question is that? I swallowed. *He's just trying to be nice. So be nice, Emily.* "Yeah, I do. But I've made some new friends here. And everyone is really nice." Just as I said these words, I recognized one of Lucas's friends Lucy. She waved to me from across the hallway and beamed. I waved back with a grin. *I was probably too enthusiastic.*

Jacob looked flabbergasted. "You just moved here, and you're already friends with Lucy Martinez?"

I blushed. "Yeah. I met her over the summer. She's friends with my neighbor." *Huh. Neighbor. It just came out. I don't usually think of Lucas as my neighbor.*

We arrived at my next class, and Jacob grinned goofily as a goodbye before he raced to go find his. The bell rang a few moments later, most likely making him late to his next period. *Much as it pains me to admit it, Jacob is pretty sweet.*

He found me again after the next class and led me to where I needed to go. He grinned his goodbye, and again was late to his next period. *Looks like this is becoming a pattern.*

At lunch, I was preparing to sit down with Jacob and all his friends from their middle school chess club when Miranda approached me.

She took me by the elbow and pulled me away from them, leaning in to whisper in my ear conspiratorially, "Those boys are nice enough, but it's social suicide to sit at their table. You seem like a fun type of girl. You are from California, after all." She giggled. "I think you'll like my friends."

I allowed myself to be led away, a forced smile on my face.

Chapter 17

By the end of the day, I was exhausted. Preseason for soccer didn't start for another couple of weeks, so I had nothing else to do but go home.

Lydia caught up with me as I wandered to the parking lot to find the car.

"So, how was your first day of high school?" She smiled at me encouragingly as we headed toward the back spots.

"Kind of boring, to be honest." I shrugged and realized she was waiting for me to ask about hers. "Oh, how was your day?"

"It was fine. I met a lot of people and joined seven different clubs. Apparently, they have a good debate program, so I joined it, too. I had my theater elective last period, so I talked a lot with the director about the plays this year. She says she's excited for me to audition and hear me sing."

"Wow, Lyds, sounds cool." The disinterest in my voice didn't seem to dissuade her.

"My classes seemed cool enough even though the options were limited because it's a smaller school. But my teachers already gave us a ton of homework. Oh, and guess what? I signed up for cross country today. Practice starts tomorrow, if you want to do it with me."

"Um, no thanks. I think I'll just stick with soccer."

"Emmy." Lydia looked a little worried. "Don't you want to get involved? It's how you meet people and make friends."

"I made friends today." I avoided her concerned gaze and stared sullenly in the distance.

"Well...yeah, but it's a little different." She clasped my shoulder and gently turned me to face her. "I know I gave you a big talk about how this year doesn't matter as much for me because I've already had all I want of the high school experience. You haven't yet."

I sighed. "Lydia, I'll be fine."

"I know. I know. Of course, you'll be fine. I just had such a good experience at our old high school and now here..." She paused as if trying to find the right words, "I just want you to have the same thing. High school is hard work, but it can be a lot of fun, too."

"Okay, Lydia. I've got it." I was starting to get irritated as we finally reached the car. "Can you open the door please?" I felt impatient, and it came out in my voice.

"I have a theater meeting about the fall production right now. I'm not leaving here for, like, another hour and a half because I'm going out afterward with a couple of the people who are trying out with me tomorrow."

"What? Then why did you walk all the way out to the car with me?"

"I don't know. I just followed you." She turned and started to go back.

"Wait. Lydia, how am I supposed to get home? Do I have to stay with you the whole time?" My voice sounded angry, even to my own ears.

"Geez, Emily, it's only an hour and a half. You can come to the meeting with me if you want."

"I want to go home. I don't want to sit with you in some stupid theater thing with all your nerdy friends."

Lydia's cheeks started to glow with telltale pink splotches. It was remarkable how much she looked like

Mom when she was upset. "Okay. You know what? I'm done. I tried to be nice and include you, but obviously you don't care." Her last words came out with a bitter sting.

I could feel my face crumpling. "Lydia, please. Can't you drive me home before you go?"

She looked a little apologetic, but she still turned to leave. "No, I'm already late. Can you please not make a scene in the parking lot? If it's really such a big deal, call Lucas and ask him to take you home."

"But it's so awkward."

"Well it's your choice. Call him or hang out with my 'nerdy friends.'" She stalked off.

I wandered out of the parking lot, resigning myself to my fate of waiting. As I sat down underneath an old oak tree, I reluctantly pulled out my phone and rolled it over in my hands as I considered. Mindlessly, I began to scroll through, finally landing upon unread texts. *Ten messages from Cora Bellville.* Guiltily, I scrolled back to our earlier conversations from the beginning of the summer. At first, they were normal enough, but gradually I began responding less and less, and all my responses were shorter and more disinterested than Cora's. Over the last couple weeks, I had barely responded at all. *What is wrong with me? It's not like Cora did anything wrong.* But I knew exactly why I had avoided. I had been distracted by another decidedly more appealing friendship.

I hadn't responded at all in two weeks. With trepidation, I scrolled down to the last text from Cora.

i don't know what i did. i don't understand why you aren't responding. i need a friend more than i ever hav in my life right now. pls call me

My heart sank as I listened to my missed voicemails, two from Cora Bellville.

"Hey Emily, it's me. It's been three days since you left, and already it feels like forever. I know you're probably busy unpacking, but call me back soon. I want to hear all about Montana. 'Kay', love ya. Bye." I barely heard the beep as the heat of shame began to creep up my neck. *I can't believe I didn't call her back.* I robotically clicked the next one.

"Emily. It's me, Cora. Your best friend. You may have forgotten me by now." Her voice stopped for a beat, wavering in a deep breath. "It's been almost three months since you left. I never hear from you anymore. At least you used to respond, however disinterested you were. But now it seems you don't care at all. Maybe time goes by faster there, but a lot can happen in three months here." She paused, for another deep breath. "I thought you should know my grandpa died a month ago." Her voice died to a whisper. "I waited for you to call, and you never did. Surely, you could never leave me in the dark for months especially through something like this, but you did." She broke into soft sobs. "It hurts a little bit more every day. The only time it doesn't is those brief moments in the early morning before I know who or where I am. It's like a punch in the gut, but it never goes away. " She stopped for a long while. "So, I guess this is goodbye, Emily. You're probably grateful this over-dramatic, crying mess on this side of the line will leave you alone now. You've most likely been waiting for this to happen for a while, so you could officially be done with me. Even still, I hope I was important enough to you for you to feel even a fraction of what I have. This is goodbye to the Emily who I used to know, because I don't even know who you are anymore." The line was silent for a while before the telltale beep.

With a jerking movement, I turned off my phone and curled up in a ball, my head resting on my knees. My insides hurt so much from the guilt that I was in physical pain. Mr. Bellville had taken the place of my biological grandfather, who had died shortly before I was born. While he hadn't been well for a while, his death was still a shock. But it was nothing compared to the shock of hearing Cora's voice again, to hearing audibly about the mistakes I had made. The pain of him being gone from this world was nothing compared to the pain of what I had done to the person who had been my closest friend for as long as I could remember. I closed my eyes to defend against the onslaught of salty tears blurring my vision. *I don't even know this new self any more than Cora does.*

My limbs were shook as I unclenched them. I couldn't sort through most of my thoughts. All I knew was I couldn't face Lydia like this. I slowly picked up my phone from where it lay alone in the grass.

Lucas answered on the third ring. "What is it? I'm driving, so I'm not supposed to be on the phone."

"You left?"

"Yeah. It's been forty-five minutes since school got out. Do you need a ride home?"

"Yeah."

"Okay, I'll turn around and pull up to the curb by the side gate. Do you know where it is?"

"Mmhmm."

"Okay, hurry. I'll be there in two minutes."

I walked quickly, but he was already waiting by the time I got there.

"Hurry before I get yelled at for illegally parking here."

I jumped in and slammed the door behind me. "Thanks, Luke. I really appreciate it."

"No problem. Why can't your sister take you home?"

"She has some stupid theater meeting." I hoped the conversation would end there, as all my aching head longed for was quiet.

"Oh. Lydia does theater?"

I sensed his surprise. People always had the same reaction when they heard Lydia did drama. Often people thought of theater kids as the high school nerdy outcasts, but Lydia defied the stereotype in almost every respect. Perfectly the opposite of me, she was tall with relatively fair skin and dark brunette hair. The only thing we shared in common was our unusual green eyes, but hers had a touch of blue. On top of being gorgeous and confident, she was also smart, some would say genius smart. People were drawn to her, though sometimes a little intimidated by her strong personality and opinions. One thing about Lydia made her stand out. Almost everyone who met her immediately liked her.

As her little sister, I didn't see all these great personality features in day-to-day life, because she certainly wasn't always friendly at home. Everyone else loved to talk about Lydia. She had been somewhat of a child prodigy back at home. It'd been easy to deduce all this about her from years of being Lydia Lawrence's little sister.

"Yeah, it feels like she does everything. But she is a particularly talented actress." I left it at that as I wasn't particularly inclined to talk about her, or anything at all really.

He kept his eyes focused on the road. "Cross country starts tomorrow, so I'm not going to be able to drive you home anymore after today."

"Seems like everyone here does cross country running," I mumbled to myself. "It's okay. Today in particular, I didn't want to stay any longer."

"Yeah, I get it. How was the rest of your day?"

"Fine. School is school."

We rode the rest of the way in silence. When we pulled up in front of my house, I said goodbye quickly and trudged inside, remembering with a pang the last time we had said goodbye in his car. I avoided my mom's questions and fell asleep the minute I collapsed on my bed.

Chapter 18

I spent the following afternoon going through all the recent social media updates from my friends back home. It was like being crushed over and over again with waves of sadness, thinking of all I had missed while I was gone. Even more sobering was seeing and remembering all the people I missed and after such a long absence, had now lost. Somehow I felt relief punishing myself for what I had done. Hanging over it all was grief and shame for my actions. Guilt rushed back as I pressed on Cora's name. She hadn't posted anything on any social media in exactly three months and three days, the day I had walked into an airplane and said goodbye to California.

"You can't hide from me forever, hon."

I jumped at the surprise of hearing a voice in my otherwise quiet room.

"Did I scare you?" Mom turned on the light. "Why is it so dark in here?"

"I dunno," I blinked at the sudden brightness. I curled into a ball and leaned against the headboard of my bed. "What are you doing in here?"

"Talking to you. You've been avoiding me, and I want to hear all about school."

"School is school." I had zero desire to talk to her.

When it became apparent I wasn't going to say anything else, she picked up the conversation again. "Lydia has perked up with school starting. Did you hear about all the clubs and activities she's joined?"

I nodded, and she continued, "I was talking to her last night, and she said yesterday was rough. But considering she's starting her senior year at a completely new school, it sounded like she's doing pretty well."

"Lydia's always been good at making friends," I muttered.

"I think distracting herself with lots of activities has been helpful." She looked hopefully at me. "I met some other moms from the welcoming committee today at the new parent coffee. Apparently, a lot of kids do cross country running, so it might be something fun for you to get involved with."

When I didn't respond, she sighed and put her hand on my knee. "Was school really so bad?"

"I told you. School was fine."

"I know freshman year can be hard..."

I interrupted roughly. "School was fine."

"Then what's wrong?"

I searched the empty air for an excuse before finally landing on something. "Mr. Bellville died."

She took a sharp breath and covered her mouth in shock. "Oh, how awful. I'm so sorry, Emmy. How's Cora?"

"She's doing great, Mom. Her beloved grandfather just died, so she's just wonderful." My words had more venom than I intended.

Mom's eyes widened in shock. "I didn't mean it like that. Of course, she must be so upset. I can't believe I didn't hear anything."

"It was relatively recent, like three weeks ago. Her family is probably keeping it quiet to process everything before they make a big announcement."

"Aw honey, I'm so sorry. I know how much time you and Cora used to spend with him." She smiled, "Probably more time at his house than ours and Cora's combined."

I returned a weak smile. "His house was so much fun. He loved showing us old movies, and telling all his old stories."

She patted my knee and stood up. "All right. I'll leave you to yourself now. Dinner's in thirty minutes."

I picked up my phone again as she started to leave. She paused before the door and gave me a sideways look. "Don't you have any homework? Lydia's been swamped."

Glancing up, I shook my head. "Lydia takes a lot harder classes than I do, so I don't have any homework yet." I tried to look convincing with this blatant lie. *The homework I have is stupid. It's the first week of school, so it doesn't really matter. And besides, she needs to stop comparing me to Lydia.*

"Okay." She looked uncertain.

My irritation got the best of me. "Why do you always compare me to Lydia?"

Mom looked slightly shocked. "I never compare you to Lydia. I was just mentioning that getting involved has been helpful for her, so I wanted to encourage you to think about trying it."

"Whatever. I'll never be as perfect as Lydia, so it doesn't even matter." I rolled my eyes and turned away.

Her eyes narrowed. "First of all, your attitude needs to stop. And secondly, Lydia is by no means perfect. I'm not telling you to get involved with the same things as Lydia. I didn't even say you should get involved at all. I mentioned it to you as an option. My comment in no way warranted this behavior."

"You know what, Mom? I'm just kind of done with this now, so can you please just go?"

"Emily Elizabeth Lawrence, do not talk to me like that. I think you're tired, so I'm going to give you some space, but I expect your attitude to improve very soon. Do you understand?"

I mumbled a response and closed my eyes, so she would leave.

Chapter 19

A couple of weeks later, Lydia decided to go in to talk to one of her teachers, so I was left to roam around campus until she finished. I wandered out to the fields and leaned against the fence separating the sports fields from the academic buildings. A small group of girls I recognized as freshman travelled past me on the other side of the fence headed to their various practices. *It should have been me and Cora starting freshman year together like them.* I felt the familiar pang. I started walking in the opposite direction from them, my hand running over the top of the metal bumps.

My mind began to wander again. *I wonder when preseason for soccer is going to start.* Out of the corner of my eye, I noticed the cross country team jogging back from their afternoon run. *Oh, God this is embarrassing. I look like such a loser hanging out watching sports practices after school.* Even as I tried to make my escape, Lucas came up from behind and tapped me on the shoulder.

He bent over panting to catch his breath. Coughing, he straightened and grinned. "So. You came to watch my practice, huh? To check out cross country?"

His cheery attitude was enough to brighten even my sullen moodiness. I gave him a bemused smile. "Not exactly. I'm waiting for Lydia, and I was bored so I came out here."

"Bummer. Cross country is fun, and you can still join if you wanted to." He looked hopeful.

I shut him down quickly. "Not gonna happen. Cross country is like a glorified version of track: running with absolutely no purpose."

He laughed. "Whatever."

We stood there awkwardly for a moment, and then an idea seemed to hit him.

"Do you want a ride home? I'm starving, so we can get food on the way."

This day is starting to get a lot better. "Yeah, I'm definitely down. Lemme text Lydia real quick, and I can go whenever you want. What kind of food were you thinking?"

"Ice cream."

"You're joking, right?"

"No. I'm completely serious. I'm hungry."

"And ice cream is always the best solution to fill an empty stomach after working out," I commented dryly.

"Yup." He walked a couple steps over and picked up his bag. "Ready?"

"Mhhm."

As we starting walking off the field, a girl began to approach. My stomach began to sink as she grew closer.

"Hey Lucas."

She was exactly as he had described her with clear, fair skin and big violet eyes. Her short spandex emphasized her long, slender legs. *I can't believe Lucas forgot to mention she was a volleyball player. Unbelievable.*

I tried to read his expression without being too obvious, but he still seemed to be in a good mood. "Hey Harper. What's up?"

Their casual exchange made it clear this was not the first time they had talked since summer. "Nothing much. Volleyball had conditioning on the field today, so that's why we're all out here."

"Nice, nice." Lucas seemed slightly uncomfortable for the first time, and lost for words.

Harper was unperturbed with one hand rested casually on her hip. "This must be the Emily I've heard all about." Her smile didn't reach her eyes.

She's beautiful and in incredible shape, and clearly she has some sort of hold still on Lucas. I could barely contain my jealousy. "Yup that's me." I levelled a steady but confident smile at her. *I really hope this is convincing.*

Luke seemed to be unable to decide what he felt about our introduction and instead stood awkwardly to the side watching us. "Um, well Emily and I are just heading for ice cream so we better get going."

"Cold Stone?"

Luke grinned. "Where else would I go to get ice cream?"

Harper laughed and rolled her eyes. "So predictable."

I just met the girl, and I still hate her.

"Well I would honestly join you two if I could because ice cream sounds so good, but I still have another thirty minutes of practice. See you later." She jogged off with her dark ponytail bouncing behind her, clearly aware Lucas was watching her.

"Okay, well, I'm hungry, so let's go." I began walking toward the parking lot.

"Good idea." Luke's eyebrows were furrowed, and he glanced back one more time.

"Something wrong?"

"No." He sighed. "It's kinda weird. Harper rarely has anything to do with me these days, and she was being really friendly back there."

Isn't it obvious? She's trying to prove to me you still belong to her. I nodded my head. "Yeah real weird." *Let's just add this to the list of my problems.*

Chapter 20

The next Saturday, I woke up in a particularly bad mood. Clutching a coffee mug between my hands, I stared blankly at the untouched page of my sketchbook on my lap. *Lucas is busy all the time, and so is Lydia. I don't have Cora to talk to anymore, and for some reason I've lost any motivation to draw. What am I doing with my life?*

Lydia burst in through the door, obviously in a rush. She raised her eyebrows at the sight of me. "You good?"

"Clearly." I muttered sarcastically.

She snorted and rolled her eyes. "Um. I'm just gonna grab my keys and leave you to get out of this funk. It's Saturday. Aren't you doing anything?"

"No."

"Good, then you'll have plenty of time to get your life back together. I get it. High school sucks, but your crappy attitude is getting annoying now." She angrily grabbed the keys sitting on the bedside table and yanked the covers off me. "Pull yourself out of it already."

It seems someone has finally noticed my mood. I sank back into my bed in self-pity. *But not the person I wanted to notice.* The one person I had wanted to talk to through this mess was Luke. But, he had become busier and busier with cross country, and it felt like he was gone all the time. *We've only hung out like twice since school started. He's the one who's partially responsible for this mess. If it weren't for him taking me everywhere all summer, I would've had more time for Cora.* I knew in the back of my mind it was completely unfair to blame everything on him, but it was nice for once to fixate my anger somewhere else. Suddenly, his name popped up on my phone, as if he'd read my mind.

hike today?

I considered for a moment before responding.

sure

It's not like I have anything better to do. I tried to maintain my anger at him, but it was difficult to ignore my anticipation at the thought of hanging out with him again.

what time? I texted.

now. I'm outside.

I jumped out of bed quickly, and pulled on some clothes. "Just like him to show up and then ask if I want to go somewhere," I muttered as I tumbled down the stairs, haphazardly throwing my knotted hair into a messy bun. He stood at the bottom of the hill, so I slowed my pace to meet him.

"Hey."

"Hi."

The exchange was awkward, so we continued on in silence.

I searched through the air to find something to talk about. "Why the sudden wakeup call this morning?"

"I don't know. I needed to talk to someone, and I wanted to hang out with you. Now seemed like a good time."

If he missed me so much, why don't we hang out as often anymore? "Why did you need someone to talk to?"

"I had a dream last night about my sister. When I woke up, it was like I was eight again, and it was Saturday morning, and we were going to go adventuring together today. And then I remembered she doesn't live at home anymore, and we haven't talked in years."

"I'm sorry. It's a rough way to wake up on a Saturday morning."

"I was thinking about missing her, and I realized I've missed you a lot, too."

He's in a weird, talkative mood. Usually I have to prod him to talk about this stuff.

Luke continued walking without looking at me. "You know, I realized something recently. Nothing really lasts. My sister and I were as close as you can imagine, and look at us now. I had the best summer of my life with you, and now..."

I felt a lump rising in my throat. *It feels like our friendship isn't lasting, either. It's like me and Cora all over again.*

"I kinda had a realization, too. I used to think some relationships didn't need much work to maintain, but all of them do." I paused for a moment. "Sometimes the ones we take for granted need the most work."

He nodded. "Yeah. I think you're right."

The sound of the crisp leaves crunching underneath every step was somehow soothing, as nature often was to me. As I walked behind Luke, the autumn hues of the trees lining the path caught my eyes. It wasn't difficult to release some of the pent-up emotion in my chest amidst the calm, quiet of the woods. I absentmindedly reached out to touch a particularly beautiful leaf with vibrant orange and brown tones, but the slight pressure from my hand caused its weak connection to the branch to break. I watched it gently float to the ground with an ominous feeling.

I suddenly broke the silence. "Isn't it funny how everyone considers fall so beautiful?"

He looked up, bemused at my outburst. "Why do you say that?"

"Everything is dead, or dying." My words brought a quick flash of pain thinking of Mr. Bellville.

"Well, there's a happy thought."

"It's true, though. We are celebrating the dying of the trees and leaves."

"I wouldn't say we *celebrate* the dying of trees and leaves. It's more like an appreciation of the beauty the colors in their final days bring to our surroundings. Besides, the trees aren't dying. They're just shedding their leaves before winter. Eventually the green returns."

"Some trees die in the winter, though." I heard the dark hint in my voice.

This time, he looked mildly concerned. "That's true, I guess. Everything dies eventually, though." I felt his gaze, as I avoided meeting his eyes. "Is everything okay?"

"Obviously." The sarcasm was apparent in my tone. *So now he notices.*

He sighed. "What's wrong?"

At his question, I suddenly felt insecure. *What am I supposed to tell him? I abandoned my closest friend from California, so I wasn't there for her when her grandpa died? I'm now walking around with the pain of losing him while simultaneously losing my oldest friend? You've been in your own little world, so you didn't even realize. And now, even our friendship is growing apart.*

"I don't know. Starting school has been hard. And you've just been so distant." Even I recognized the accusation in my tone.

"I've been working through some things." His tone was soothing and mild, but the dissatisfaction and anger seething in my gut took it as disinterest. "Remember, relationships are two-sided. Both sides need to work to maintain them, just like you were talking about. But, I should have been a better friend these past few weeks. I'm sorry."

"Are you really? I needed you this past couple weeks, and you weren't there."

I could see his eyes darkening. "I said I was sorry."

"These days, I don't know if you even value our friendship sometimes."

"Now, you're just picking a fight."

"You asked what was wrong."

"We both know this isn't what's wrong. You're upset about something, and you're turning your anger on me because I'm an easy target."

The frankness and truthfulness of his words stopped me for a moment. "You don't know that."

"Have you even thought for a second that maybe that this friendship hasn't been easy for me, either? You've been carrying around some sort of problem you won't talk to me about. You don't have to tell me everything. We all have problems we keep close, but you have been nursing this one for weeks now. You're in a bad mood all the time." He threw up his hands in frustration. "Earlier, I was trying to open up about missing my sister, which is a personal problem I deal with to encourage you to open up too. You know how much I hate talking about my sister. And yet, you still didn't open up."

It's because I don't know how to talk about it. If I do, you'll think I'm a terrible friend and think less of me. And the longer I don't tell you, the more irritated you get with me. "I'm sorry, okay?"

He stopped and turned to face me. "You don't even know what you want anymore. You've had this lost, puppy-dog look in your eyes for days. You think I didn't notice?"

My eyes widened at his controlled anger.

"Well, I did. You're sulking about school all the time when you're there and when you're not. You refuse to get involved. It's like..." He struggled for the right words, "It's like you don't even know who you are anymore." He looked at me, and this time it wasn't with anger, but empathy. For a second, I wanted to forgive him. His words struck a chord I didn't know existed. It was silent for a moment as I tried to process. *He's right. I don't know who I am.* But his being right meant so much more was wrong with me.

He sighed and ran his fingers through his hair in frustration. "You're dwelling on superficial things, but you aren't diving deeper because you don't know what's there. It's kind of like you're—lost."

This was too much. "You know what? I'm done with this hike. We go on these stupid walks all the time."

The air was still, devoid of all wind and all sound for a moment.

"If I'd known you didn't like them, I wouldn't have asked." His eyes flashed, yet he couldn't hide the injured tone.

No, Luke, I'm sorry. I didn't mean it. But somehow, I couldn't say the words aloud.

The sinking feeling in the pit of my stomach was all too familiar. Nothing came out of my mouth, so I simply watched him go with overwhelming confusion on top of the lake of emotion pooling behind my eyes. *Why did I say that? What am I even doing right now?* As soon as he was out of sight, my insides began to crumple.

Somehow, when things start going wrong, everything else seems to follow suit all at once.

Chapter 21

Two afternoons later, I found myself sitting in the back of the auditorium. I ran my fight with Luke over and over in my head, wishing more than anything it had gone differently. I came up with dozens of scenarios, dozens of different things I could have said to make the result different. As easy as it was to be mad at him, I knew I was in the wrong, and all of me wanted our friendship to be right again.

Miss Melody, the young but passionate director was yelling at the small group of auditioners onstage. "None of you are right for this part. I need someone younger. Do you know anyone else who might be interested in doing this production?" She turned to search the auditorium. "Hey you back there, what's your name?"

I shrank back into my chair. "Umm..."

Lydia answered for me. "That's my little sister, Emily. She's a freshman."

"You're the age I need for this part. Have you ever seen *Fiddler on the Roof?*"

I turned red. "Well, yeah." *I am Lydia's sister after all. She's forced me to watch like every Broadway movie ever.*

"Please come up here and sing this part for me."

I set my homework aside. Every inch of me was quaking and protesting as I slowly walked up. "Um, Miss Melody, I don't really sing."

"Humor me. Lydia, sing the eldest sister's part. Victoria, come sing the second oldest. Emily, you will sing the third daughter's."

I swallowed hard, and my eyes pleaded with Lydia to help me.

Everyone on stage watched me with curiosity as I walked up the steps. Miss Melody handed me the music and played my notes on the piano. Lydia began and sang beautifully as always, while she also managed to incorporate the accent. Victoria sang quietly, but her voice sounded low and soulful. My voice cracked on the first note out of my mouth.

Miss Melody stopped playing. "Try again."

I cleared my throat. My voice was quiet at first, but slowly it gained volume as the song went on. Lydia and Victoria joined me for the harmony, and my soprano notes soared high above theirs, sweet even to my own untrained ears. Our perfectly blended voices gave me chills. When we finished, the auditorium was silent for an instant before everyone began to clap enthusiastically.

Miss Melody beamed. "Perfect. Emily, I just knew you would have a good voice after hearing your sister sing."

Lydia smiled proudly. "To be quite honest, I didn't really know she could sing. She never does at home."

Miss Melody looked thoughtful. "She certainly has a very different voice from yours."

I shuffled my feet uncomfortably and felt my cheeks turn red.

"Anyway, thank you all for auditioning today. Roles and schedules will be posted first thing tomorrow morning. Rehearsals will start tomorrow as well."

I went to the back of the auditorium to grab my stuff before I walked out with Lydia.

"Well, well, well. Who knew my baby sister could sing?" Lydia grinned as we headed toward the car.

"Yeah, well I didn't." I gave her a half smile. "It's so ironic. The director's name is Melody."

"I asked someone about it. Apparently, she came from a musical family. Her sister is named Lyric."

I laughed aloud. "It's actually pretty clever."

Lydia joined in. "If she had a brother, they could have named him Forte."

"Eww." I giggled. "By the way, your theater friends aren't as bad as I thought."

"I told you." She smiled smugly. "You might be hanging out with them a lot more than you realize. You made a pretty good impression on Miss Melody."

"I doubt it. They wouldn't give a freshman a lead."

Chapter 22

We were quiet on the drive home. Every time I looked out at the brown and gold leaves, I was reminded of my fight with Lucas.

"Why so pensive, sis? You had an excellent audition."

"I'm just thinking." Something drove me to go further. "Lydia?"

"Yeah?" She kept her eyes on the road ahead.

"Do you think I'm lost?"

Lydia raised her eyebrows at the bluntness of the question. "Interesting question. Why do you ask?"

"Um, Luke said something about it the other day. We sorta got into a fight."

"Ah, I see. Trouble in paradise, huh?"

I snorted. "It's far from paradise."

"Lost? I guess it's one way of putting it."

"So, you do think I'm lost?"

"I would say you are definitely going through something. I don't think it's just because your freshman year isn't going as well as you'd hoped. I think something happened, and you aren't sharing it with anyone. Yes., I'd say you're lost." She paused for a moment, far away in thought as she kept her hands steady on the steering wheel. "Lost perhaps not in the way you're thinking. Lost as in you don't know exactly who you are. It's the beginning of high school. You just moved to a new place. You're with new people, and you're trying to figure out the kind of person you want to be now. You're not a kid anymore, and dramatic changes in your life have forced you to rethink who you want to be seen as."

I sat quietly, thinking about what she'd said. "I think you pretty much got it, much as it pains me to admit it."

"I usually am," she replied smugly.

I smiled absentmindedly in response.

She turned to glance at me for a second. "The best solution is age old: time. It takes time to sort yourself out. But you do have to try." She laughed a bit. "You tend to dwell. In all seriousness, though, I will share these following words of wisdom."

I cut her off with a laugh. "Oh wise one, do share."

"Do not question the wise sage. I was *going* to say—" She sobered up. "You'll find it difficult to find true success and joy in relationships if you don't know yourself. You become so close you forget where you stop and the other person begins."

We both knew exactly who she was talking about.

She continued, "And when you pop your head back in the real world, as we all have to do eventually, you'll inevitably find yourself—lost."

My face began to heat up with the full realization of what she was saying.

As we pulled into the driveway, Lydia finished with a sigh and long glance at me. "Unfortunately, summers never lasts forever."

Chapter 23

By the next morning, I had resolutely decided I was going to get myself unlost. By first period, I was already confused as to how to go about it. While I remained in confusion, I had firmly locked away all thoughts of Cora.

"I think congratulations are in order." Jacob turned around at his desk and gave me a solemn nod.

"Uh, for what?"

"Didn't you check the cast list this morning outside the auditorium?"

"Oh, you mean for theater? No, I forgot."

I saw Miranda turn to listen with a poor attempt at subtlety.

Jacob tried to hide his surprise. "You got one of the leads, Tevya's third daughter."

"I did?" I felt the color drain from my face. *I'm not an actress. I can't do this. Besides, I don't even like theater.*

"Yeah. You don't look as excited as you should be."

"No, I am. I'm just...surprised I guess." I paused. "Why were you checking the cast lists?"

"Well, actually, I tried out. Didn't you see me there yesterday?"

"Well, no. But did you get anything?"

Jacob turned slightly red. "Well I got the part of Fiedka."

"Who's that?" I responded bluntly.

He turned even redder. "Um, your love interest."

I tried to contain my shock. *This is crazy. I got a part. Now everyone is going to think of me as a weird theater kid. Plus, Jacob is my love interest? This whole thing must be some kind of joke.* "Wow. Fantastic."

Chapter 24

After class, Miranda walked up from behind and linked arms with me as had become her habit. "Theater, huh? Who would've known?" I detected the snub in her tone.

"My sister got me into it." Jacob was right behind me, preventing me from saying anything rude about theater, which Miranda obviously expected.

"And Jacob's your love interest?" This time she laughed outright.

Jacob, please turn the other way. I closed my eyes and mentally tried to cue him to leave. I simply nodded my head in response to Miranda.

"Any onstage kisses in your future?" She just wouldn't leave it alone.

I hoped this couldn't get any worse. But of course, it did.

"Probably will be the only time the poor nerd gets any bit of action. The guy obviously has a huge crush on you."

This proved to be too much for Jacob. Hurrying past us, he nearly dropped the books in his arms. The look of shock on Miranda's face was replaced by peals of laughter.

"I can't believe he heard us." At this point, Miranda nearly doubled over.

"I can't believe you said it." I angrily pulled my arm away. "You embarrassed the poor kid."

"Who cares? I was joking. Mostly." She snorted with laughter and derision at her own joke.

It had become apparent that Miranda enjoyed me as a friend because of the status it gave her. People at the school couldn't get over the fact I was from California. But finally, this was enough. "You know what? Jacob's a nice guy. He's a good friend, unlike some people. And for your information, I like the theatre people, as uncool as they are in your unnecessary opinion."

Her face barely had time to register shock before I quickly disappeared into the crowds surrounding us.

Chapter 25

After school, I found my way to the cast list hanging on the door of the auditorium. *This is unbelievable. How did this even happen? I am not ready for this.*

"So. Word around town is the cute little freshman from California got a lead in the play, and on the same day she told off a certain freshman to defend the theater kids." Lydia's voice broke me from my thoughts.

My cheeks warmed. "How did you find out?"

"I have my ways." She winked.

"Seriously, though. How?"

"There are about thirty of us in drama. We're a tight group. Word gets around quickly." She raised her voice to a falsetto. "Emily, you're our hero, defending us unpopular theater nerds from the mean freshman." Her voice returned to normal.

I snorted and rolled my eyes. Lydia couldn't care less about her social status at school or any of her friends' either. "You guys aren't *that* nerdy."

She laughed. "I take offense. I love being a nerd. But on a more serious note, congratulations are in order for my sister, the new star of Bozeman High School's production of *Fiddler on the Roof.*"

"Thanks, but you got one of main leads. You're the one to be congratulated."

She smiled, but the praise simply bounced off her shoulders.

Chapter 26

When we arrived home that evening, Lydia seemed to be in a better mood than usual. She burst through the door with a grin on her face. "Mom," she called. "Guess what?"

"What?" My mother peeked her head out of the office.

Lydia was practically beaming. "Ems and I got lead roles in the school play."

Mom's eyebrows went shooting up. "Emily, I didn't know you tried out. I'm so proud of you, hon."

My sister's smile slowly began to turn into a scowl. "Gee, thanks."

"Lydia, I'm proud of you too, but this isn't out of the ordinary for you."

Of course, perfect Lydia.

"Well, still. It's kinda rude to congratulate Ems and completely ignore me."

"I didn't mean it like that. Emily hasn't exactly been—" Mom hesitated and her eyes flickered toward me. "Well, she hasn't been excited to get involved."

"Mom," I protested. "I just moved to a new state, and I'm starting high school for the first time."

Lydia suddenly turned toward me. "It's a new state and a new school for all of us. You can't use it as an excuse forever."

Her criticism was like a punch in the gut. I shot Lydia an accusatory look. *I thought you were on my side.*

"I'm the one who's suffered the most with this move. And I'm also the one who's adjusted the best. But nobody's' praising me for doing a good job of 'getting involved.'" Lydia's scowl deepened.

"It's different for you, Lydia. We're not the same person, you know." My normally calm voice was tense.

"Girls, stop it. It's been hard for everyone. I'm happy for both of you." Mom stepped in to try to play peacemaker.

"Mom, you don't understand anything." Lydia's normally bright eyes darkened. "I'm so tired of all this. I can't wait to leave and go to college."

My mother's face dropped as Lydia stalked off. I gave her a sympathetic look before I slipped out the back door to sit on the porch steps. I pulled out my phone and realized with a pang, *I can't text Lucas anymore.* Hugging my knees to my chest, I shivered in the cool evening air. There was no summer breeze to warm me.

Chapter 27

"All right cast." Miss Melody clapped for our attention. "Everybody quiet down and take a seat."

I tried to hide in the back corner of the auditorium behind a book.

"Come up here and sit by me," Lydia whispered in my ear and tugged my arm.

I looked up at her in surprise. *Um, I thought she was still mad at me.*

She must have read my expression because she shrugged and gave me a small smile. I stood up and followed her down the aisle. *I swear it feels like everyone is staring at me.*

"I'm going to have the schedules out to you all by tomorrow. Bryce is handing out scripts now for the read-through today." Miss Melody bustled around the stage, pointing directions to the stage managers.

"What's a read-through?" I said quietly into Lydia's ear.

Her eyes opened in surprise. "It's when we read through the script."

I suddenly felt very small in my seat. *Oh no. I didn't realize we were doing so much today. It's only the first rehearsal.*

"Don't worry about it. Miss Melody won't be too harsh on you. She understands you're not used to all this." A girl on the other side of me smiled comfortingly.

Voices of various students around me began to speak in turn.

What have I gotten myself into now? My panicked heart began to thud faster.

Lydia nudged me.

I couldn't move.

She nudged me again. "Emily go. It's your line."

I can't do this. The words barely escaped my throat.

"Emily, you need to speak up, please. It's a read-through, but you still need to put some emotion into it." Miss Melody looked at me with raised eyebrows.

I nodded my head.

"Try again." She gave me a small smile.

I repeated the line again, louder and with more confidence. This time, she didn't stop us.

"Nice," Lydia whispered into my ear.

I let out a long breath, and prepared for my next line. *You can do this, Emily.*

Chapter 28

"All principal characters need to go to the wardrobe room after school today," a girl's voice called from the side of the auditorium stage.

All of us on stage looked to see who was talking.

Is that Lucy, Luke's friend?

"Emily? Is it you? What are you doing back here?" Lucy beamed at me.

Lydia looked back and forth between us with a confused expression.

"A couple of us are running through some lines." I smiled back at her.

Some of the other kids returned to looking at their scripts, but I knew they were all listening.

"Oh, very cool. I didn't know you were doing the play."

"Yeah." I turned and gave Lydia a wry smile. "I was kind of roped into it, actually."

"Awesome. Well, I do costuming, so I'll see you after rehearsal to get your measurements."

"Sounds good." I gave her one last smile before turning back to my script.

She left through the wings of the stage. Miss Melody resumed staging the opening monologue with Tevya.

I let out a long breath. *I can't believe Lucy's even talking to me, especially after what happened between me and Lucas. He probably told her everything.*

"How do you know Lucy Martinez?" Lydia's eyes appraised me.

I didn't look up. "Um, I met her over the summer. She's friends with Luke."

"Got it."

I could feel Lydia's eyes watching me.

"How's Luke doing by the way?"

"I think he's fine." *Why is she still talking about this?*

"You think?" She questioned.

I sighed. "We haven't exactly talked in a while."

"Since your last argument?" Lydia raised her eyebrows.

"Yes." I flipped the page of my script. "Can we please keep running through these lines?"

"Sure. But I think we should talk about this later."

I think maybe not.

Chapter 29

As Lydia and I walked out of rehearsal, I noticed Luke and Harper walking ahead of us in the parking lot. Something in my heart burned.

Lydia turned and gave me a look, but I refused to acknowledge it.

Harper leaned her head back and laughed. "Oh my God, I miss these conversations so much." Her voice trailed behind her, reaching my ears.

I'll bet you do. I couldn't hear Luke's response, but it warranted a smile from Harper. My heart ached. *I miss him so much.*

"This is my truck here. See you later, Harper."

"See ya."

As he turned to unlock his door, he glanced behind him and stopped. Our eyes met for a brief moment, but he quickly opened his door and climbed into the driver's seat.

I looked the other way and tried to compose myself. *Don't cry. Don't cry. Don't cry.* Lydia and I continued on to our car in silence, but she turned and gave me a look the minute we were both inside.

"What the heck was that about?"

I looked out the passenger window and tried to swallow the lump in my throat. "I don't want to talk about it."

Chapter 30

A few weeks later, Miranda turned from her desk to talk to me. "Where were you yesterday?"

"What was yesterday?" I was so tired I could barely focus on her voice. *I cannot believe rehearsal ended two hours late last night. It's so ridiculous.*

"Um, you missed soccer tryouts."

My heart dropped. *What? How could this have happened?* "Oh no. When was the date posted?"

"It was on the morning announcements. Looks like you won't be able to play this season. Too bad." Miranda turned back in her seat and faced the teacher.

Stupid theater practice. I can't believe I missed the tryouts. This sucks.

Jacob approached me after class to walk to lunch with me. "Is everything okay?"

Am I really so transparent? I let out a long breath. "I missed soccer tryouts yesterday, and I'm super bummed."

His eyebrows furrowed. "Oh yeah. I forgot you played soccer."

"Mhhm." I was so completely preoccupied with my thoughts I almost didn't hear Jacob talking to me again.

"Well, I know you are super bummed about soccer, but would you want to walk with me after school and grab some frozen yogurt or something to cheer you up? My house is super close too, so I was thinking we could run over some lines and stuff."

Is Jacob asking me out on a date? The anticipation and nervousness in his expression gave me all the answer I needed. *Oh no. This is so awkward. Jacob's nice and everything, but I could never think of him in that way. Lydia would kill me if I said no, though. Besides, he's been a good friend, so I owe it to him to at least hang out once.*

Just then, I noticed Luke walking ahead of me with Harper and a few other people. *Harper and Luke seem to be together all the time now. I wonder if they're dating again.* The thought was so disconcerting I shoved it aside. "Um, I don't think I have anything after school today," I responded to Jacob, but my eyes never left Luke.

He handed me a tray as we got in line for lunch together. "So...?"

"Yeah, sure. Sounds like fun."

Chapter 31

"So do you like theater so far?"

I looked up at Jacob from my frozen yogurt and tried to appear interested in the conversation. "Um, yeah. It hasn't been too bad."

He nodded, and seemed to search for another question to ask. "That's good. Are you nervous for the dress rehearsals coming up?"

"Yeah." I nodded my head vigorously. "I don't even want to think about it."

He laughed at my terrified expression. "It's not bad. Being in costume actually kinda helps."

I found myself laughing with him. "Since when did you become a theater veteran?" A new thought stabbed my heart. *This should be Lucas across the table from me, not Jacob.*

He grinned sheepishly and blushed. "I did a play or two in middle school."

I giggled. "Don't lie. I can tell from your expression you did more than that."

"It may have been more like five or six." He looked down wryly at his frozen yogurt.

I raised my eyebrows and smiled. "So you *are* a theater veteran."

"Well, not exactly." He blushed again as he got up to throw his bowl away. "If you're done, I can take yours, too."

"Oh, thanks." I watched as he walked over to the trashcan. *I wonder if how I feel about Jacob is like how*

Lucas feels about me. He enjoyed being friends, but I followed him around like a lovesick puppy.

"Ready to run some lines?" He looked at me expectantly.

My smile was more confident than I felt inside. "Yup. Remember, I've never been in a play before, much less performed any sort of romantic role." *Gosh, this is going to be so awkward.*

He grinned. "Don't worry about it at all. I'll help you."

Chapter 32

"Emily, you're almost through memorizing your lines, right?" Lydia asked from her bed, the computer lighting up her face.

"Um..." I looked up from my sketch. *Sort of?*

"Miss Melody wants us pretty much off book by tomorrow."

Looks like I won't be doing any homework tonight after all. I looked guiltily at my backpack sitting on the floor next to me. *I can't remember the last time I actually finished my math homework. Cora always used to help me with this stuff.* My heart jumped into my throat again.

I checked my phone, but I had no notifications. *When am I going to stop waiting for texts from Lucas?*

"How was your date with Jacob?" Lydia tried to sound casual.

"Fine," I mumbled.

"He's a good guy."

"A very good *friend*," I emphasized.

"Still hung up over Lucas, huh?"

"Lydia." I nearly threw my pillow at her. "Don't be ridiculous."

"I'm not being ridiculous. You're the one in denial."

"Gee, thanks. Now I feel even worse."

"Aw, don't be so sensitive. I'm only helping you here."

"No, you're not." I rolled my eyes. "I don't want to talk about Lucas. Okay?"

"Fine, fine," she muttered. "Obviously you are doing a fantastic job getting over him by yourself."

"Just because I only think of Jacob as a friend doesn't mean I'm not over Lucas." I angrily flipped through the pages of my script.

"It's not just that. You're constantly checking your phone to see if he's texting you."

I opened my mouth to argue, but she cut me off.

"It's not like Cora's texting you anymore."

I felt like another knife stabbed my gut.

"You think I didn't notice?" Lydia looked at me with a superior expression.

I clenched my jaw.

"She probably got tired of you ignoring her for Lucas."

Now she's just baiting me. Don't answer.

"And Jacob doesn't have a phone, so he's not texting you. The other theater kids wouldn't be texting you, and you really don't have friends outside of them. So that just leaves Lucas." She stopped for dramatic effect. "But clearly, he hasn't been texting you either."

"You know what, Lydia? Just shut up," I yelled across the room at her. I took a deep breath to calm myself, and my voice turned cold. "It's not like there've been any notifications from Finn popping up on your phone recently either, so you're one to talk." The minute I said it, I knew I had gone too far.

Her face dropped. "That was low."

I swallowed and refused to respond.

"Well, goodnight, I guess."

I nodded my head and tried to hold in the tears, which threatened to burst.

Chapter 33

"Emily." My mother's face was more serious than usual.

Uh oh. "Yeah, Mom?"

"I just got emails from two of your teachers saying you haven't been turning in homework. What's this about?"

Oh boy. Homework and school had been the last of my worries recently. "Um, I'm still getting used to high school." It had become easier and easier to lie to my mother.

She gave me a long look. "I expect better reports in the future, Emily. Do you understand?"

"Yes," I replied meekly.

Liam peeked his head in. "Mom, you're supposed to be reading to me right now."

"I have to go. Goodnight, Emily."

"Goodnight."

I heard Lydia's voice from the hallway. "Mom, he's eight. Shouldn't he be reading by himself now?"

"No," came her abrupt answer. "He's the baby. I'll read to him as long as he wants."

"You can't pretend he's five forever."

Of course, Lydia has to have the last word.

She walked in soon after. As soon as Mom was out of hearing proximity, Lydia looked at me with her usual raised eyebrows. "What was that about?"

"Oh just Mom being Mom." Lydia had no concept of what a struggle school was for me. She took an impossible schedule while always seeming to maintain straight As and a constant cool.

"Gotcha." She started to change from her school clothes into pajamas. "I'm sorry about the other night."

"It's fine."

"I shouldn't have said all those things, especially about Cora and Lucas."

"I shouldn't have said what I did about Finn." I stood up from my bed and looked out the window.

"What exactly happened with you and Cora?"

"You pretty much said it. I've barely responded to her, and she got fed up with me. Mr. Belville died," I added quietly. "And I wasn't there for her. She had a total right to be angry with me."

"Did you call her back?" I heard her quietly getting into bed.

"No. I didn't know what to say."

It was quiet for a while. Tonight seemed different from most nights. It was the beginning of November, and the weather had cooled off considerably, so only my thoughts prevented me from rest. Since I couldn't fall asleep, I stayed awake. My elbows rested on the windowsill. The window was wide open, but the curtains remained still. No breeze moved them. I leaned my head out and looked up at the sky. The last glimmers of sunlight had disappeared beyond the horizon, but no light was needed. Even compared to glimmering stars, the full moon's brilliance and pale beauty far outshone anything else in the night. While the sun could be harsh and unrelenting, the moon had a glow all its own, a peace and stillness the sun could never duplicate.

In moments like these, I felt small and overwhelmed by the beauty in the world. I felt closest to myself and to my thoughts. In the silence around me, I heard everything running through my mind. What stood out most was not nervousness about the play, or even missing California. It was loneliness. It seemed slightly ridiculous. I had friends at school and a family who loved me. *I have no extraordinary gifts or talents to set me apart from other people, and no real reason to feel depressed or lost. I've separated myself from my old life in California, and yet, I still haven't found what Mom wanted me to find by moving away, whatever it was.*

I'm probably not the only one. It hit me suddenly, the realization no one ever would know my mind and thoughts, look inside and fully understand everything that made me myself. The most anyone else could do is look at me from the outside and talk to the part of me I showed to the world.

Beyond everything was the thought of Cora. The guilt weighed on me almost as much as the loneliness. *But I don't want to think about her.*

Though these realizations weighed on me as I gazed at the moon, trying to memorize each facet and discernable crevice, a different kind of loneliness pulled at me as well. *I miss Luke.* I rubbed my face with my hands and tucked away a stray piece of hair. *I miss our friendship, those tingly feelings when I first started to realize how much I liked him, all the adventures we went on together. But mostly, I miss him because he is the only true best friend I have left. He was my person, and he's gone now.* This pulled at me the most, this war between friendship and something more, something close to love.

"Emily, you really should get some sleep. Our first performance is tomorrow."

My sister's voice shook me out of my thoughts. "I can't sleep."

Without looking, I heard her sit up and come to stand next to me.

"What are you thinking about?" Her voice was soft, barely more than a whisper.

"A lot of things. But mostly...mostly Luke."

"You miss him, don't you?"

"He's one of the best friends I've ever had. Maybe I'm dramatic, but I feel like I've lost him." I sighed and rested my head in my hands. "I'm only fifteen. He's the only guy I've ever really liked, so maybe I'm letting my emotions get the best of me. I just feel so lonely and lost and confused and all these other emotions I can't quite put my finger on."

Lydia's quiet laugh surprised me. "Of course, you aren't being dramatic. Everyone is lonely to some extent because no two people on earth are exactly the same. It's normal. We're teenage girls, remember? You can't even imagine how many times I've been there."

It's hard to imagine Lydia as a normal teenage girl. "I know." I looked out at the trees surrounding our house. "This is going to sound crazy, but don't you ever wish you could meet your soulmate right now?"

"You really need to go to bed."

"You know what I mean. Don't you wish you could skip all the pain of stupid crushes and meet the person you'll get to love forever?"

She was quiet for a long time. "I guess."

"Lydia?" My voice was almost childlike in its simplicity.

"Mhhm?"

"Do you...do you still miss Finn? Do you talk to him at all now?"

I thought I imagined it for a moment, but a glimmer of loneliness shined in Lydia's eyes. "Of course I miss him," she said softly.

It was eerie, hearing the strong voice of my sister, who had spoken in front of hundreds of people, sung powerful songs, fought intense debates, reduced to just a whisper. "I think about him all the time. We talk once in a while. It's not as easy to let go of someone you care a lot for as you might think."

"But isn't it awkward? I mean, you broke up."

"In my opinion, breakup can be a misleading word. It can take one conversation to officially break up the relationship, but the emotional break up can last for months if not years. For some people, it lasts a lifetime. When you genuinely care about someone, Emmy, a part of them stays with you even after the relationship is over." She sighed. "And I dated—no, I loved Finn for a long time. I still do."

Some part of me was frightened, seeing my strong sister this vulnerable. "Do you still miss California?"

"Why do you ask?"

"Recently you've acted so at home here in Montana. And you haven't fought with Mom about going home in a while."

"Montana will never be home for me. I grew up in California. My home will always be there. But my family is here. It's like you said, having things to do doesn't solve your problems, but it's a good distracter." She was quiet again for a while. "What about you?"

"I miss California. I don't think I ever let myself grieve leaving there like you did over the summer. Luke was my distraction. But now, it's hitting me. I miss our old house and the beach and my soccer team, but I think I miss the people there the most, and the person I used to be. Life was a lot easier for her. And since I've lost Luke, I miss him, too."

Lydia didn't say anything. Her arm around my shoulder was enough.

"I've been thinking a lot tonight..."

"I can tell. You're very philosophical."

"This is going to sound crazy, but sometimes listening to my own thoughts, and talking to you of course, makes me a little less lonely."

"It isn't crazy at all."

Out of the corner of my eye, I saw the curtain flutter slightly and the cool breeze washed over my face, covering me in goosebumps. I closed my eyes and breathed in the piney smell of the woods. If I closed my eyes, I could almost imagine Luke right next to me with his arm around me instead of my sister's. "I think I'm ready to go to sleep now."

"You and your weird thing with the wind." She rolled her eyes and climbed back into her bed.

"Love you, Lydia. Goodnight." I snuggled into my warm blankets.

"Love you, too."

Chapter 34

As the curtains closed on our first dress rehearsal, I breathed a huge sigh of relief.

"You did good, baby sister," Lydia whispered into my ear. "Are you feeling ready?"

"Sort of," I said queasily.

Miss Melody clapped her hands as the curtains opened again. "Great job tonight, everyone. We still have a few tech things to work out, but otherwise you all did a fantastic job. Leads, come see me after you are out of costumes and make up. I have a few notes for you."

I rushed with everyone to the wardrobe room, eager to get out of my stuffy dress.

Lucy unzipped me. "So, how are you feeling about everything?"

I smiled. "Not too bad. I think I did all right tonight. I need to go over some staging with Jacob for our scene, but otherwise, I felt good."

"Great." She helped me step out of my dress, and tipped her head a tad as she smiled at me. "When this is all over, let's go get a coffee or something and catch up."

"Sounds perfect to me."

Chapter 35

As we took our final bows on the last night, I felt my cheeks flush with pride. *I did it.* I certainly wasn't the star of the performance. Lydia took the title. I had done my best, and by the looks on my parents' faces, it was pretty good. Maybe it wasn't quite as fun as soccer, but it came pretty darn close. Right before the final curtain fell, one smiling face stood out from the crowd: Luke.

After thanking Miss Melody and getting out of our costumes, we were excused. Luke looked uncertain as I flew into his arms. "You came."

He hugged me awkwardly. "What kind of friend would I be if I didn't come to your debut as an actress?" He smiled, but the emotion in his eyes was hard to discern.

I gave him one last grateful smile before I was pulled away by my chattering, excited family. I turned around and mouthed, "I've missed you."

"Text me," he called back.

When I finally got a chance, I checked my phone. Luke had already texted me.

I missed u too. wanna do something this weekend?

a hike sounds good to me :)

Chapter 36

I tucked a strand of hair behind my ear as I made my way through the busy hallway, crammed with bodies becoming increasingly familiar as I walked to the same classes day after day. Suddenly, someone I knew well appeared out of the crowd. I felt my face light up. "Hey Luke."

"Hey Emily," he responded casually before continuing on.

Confused, I turned around as he walked past me and watched as he disappeared without looking back. All I could do was keep going.

~ ~ ~

Later that day, Lucy approached me. "Emily, I'm so glad I found you. I was hoping we could pin down a date for us to get coffee or something."

I smiled. "Hey Lucy. Yeah, with the play over, I'm available these days."

"Okay, awesome." She grinned. "How is everything? I noticed Lucas came to see you in the play."

"Yeah, I was super stoked, but he was acting kinda distant again this morning."

"Hmm, tell you what. I have to go right now, but let's do coffee after school today. Does it work for you?"

"Perfect."

"Okay cool, I'll text you where to meet me."

Chapter 37

"So, he barely responded, and just kept going?"

"Yeah, and he avoided me the rest of the day."

Lucy looked perplexed. "How weird." She laughed. "I wish I could just say boys are weird, but Lucas is especially confusing."

"Yeah." I laughed. "I figured it one out pretty early on."

She hesitated before continuing. "You know, I meant to tell you something earlier in the year, but for some reason I forgot. I'm so glad we're finally getting the chance to talk now, even though it's November already."

"Me too." I smiled, but the slight concern in her eyes was unsettling.

"I've known Lucas for a long time, and he's a really good guy." She giggled. "I even had a crush on him in sixth grade. But he can be very on and off." She paused to study my expression.

"Yeah, so I've noticed."

"Like he'll get very close with people quickly, and then he'll withdraw just as quickly. Most people wouldn't realize this about him, but he's actually still learning a lot about friendship. He's a great guy, but he keeps to himself a lot, with a few exceptions, obviously." She looked out the window of the cute coffee shop we were in. "I've talked to Jack extensively about this, and he thinks it started after Luke's sister left. He used to be a lot more social before then. They were best friends, totally inseparable, and I think her absence has affected him more than we realized."

"It's interesting." I was quiet for a moment. "He's only talked about her a few times to me."

"I wouldn't worry about it. I know you guys have gone through a rough patch recently, but you'll get through it."

I really hope so. "Lucy, can I ask you something?"

"Of course."

"Are Harper and Luke dating again?"

She laughed aloud. "Heck, no. They may look like they're friends, but it's just because Harper likes to keep up appearances. If anybody so much as bats an eyelash at him, she's all over him suddenly. But Harper doesn't care about anybody except Harper, and she gets bored with people too quickly to date. She used him last year just to prove something." Lucy snorted with disgust. "But I have no idea what Luke thinks of her now."

"Didn't they mutually break up?"

"God, no." She looked up me with an amused expression. "Where are you getting your information?"

"Luke." I shrugged.

"No, it was definitely not mutual. Harper decided she was tired of having a boyfriend and dumped him."

I was dumbfounded. "Why would she do that? She's been all over him this year."

"She only cares about herself, remember? She got bored with him. But Harper is the possessive type, so as soon as she found out the two of you had gotten close over the summer, she entered the picture again."

"That's ridiculous."

"That's Harper for you."

Trust the Wind

Chapter 38

hey r u okay?
I sent the text to Luke later the same night.
yeah
His response came almost immediately.
u were acting kinda weird today
i was? sorry
it's fine I was just wondering if something was wrong
nah. gtg I have hw
I set down my phone on the porch step next to me with a sigh and tried to shake off the nagging feeling I was getting. *At least tomorrow is Saturday. Maybe I can talk to him while we're on our hike.*
"What are you thinking about?" Lydia's voice surprised me.
"Stuff."
She sat down next to me on the porch steps.
"What are you doing?" I turned to face her.
"Escaping."
"Argument with Mom?"
"Yup."
"I didn't hear it, so it couldn't have been too bad."
"Dad took Liam upstairs to our parents' room and started playing *Star Wars* really loudly to distract the poor kid. You know how he hates it when we fight."
"So, it was a bad one."
"Pretty brief, but bloody all the same."

Page 131

"When are you ever going to stop arguing with Mom?"

"When she starts being reasonable."

I couldn't help but smile. "Fat chance of that. Your definition of reasonable is different than most."

"So what were you thinking about?"

"Guess."

"Luke."

"I hate it when you guess right."

"You'll have to stop asking me to guess then." She paused. "What about Luke?"

"It's just—It seems like everything is going well. School has gotten into a rhythm, of sorts. I feel like myself, and I'm happier than I've been for months. I thought Luke and I were working things out, and then he does something weird today, and he throws me for a loop again. Maybe I'm over-thinking things." My heart twinged. *And then there's still Cora.*

"Don't let him control your emotions so much."

I snorted with laughter. "Easier said than done."

"Remember when he said you were lost?"

"Yeah, but I think I've kind of found myself now."

"I agree. That wasn't where I was going. Have you ever thought maybe Luke is a little lost, too?"

"Maybe." It was hard to imagine Luke being lost.

"What else is it?"

"What?"

"I know there's something else."

"It's Cora, still."

Lydia sighed. "Why don't you try talking to her?"

"What's the point? She doesn't want to talk to me."

"You don't know for sure." Lydia shrugged. "Might as well try."

"Maybe."

Lydia stood up. "Well, I think I've had enough time to cool off. I have to face the flames eventually."

"Lydia, you are the flames. Don't go in there and start another argument with Mom. It gets you nowhere every time."

"If you fail and don't succeed, try, try again."

"That is a terrible application of the saying."

She shrugged. "At least if it gets me nowhere and my rights as a person in this family remain forgotten, I'll be an excellent debater someday."

"Fantastic," I muttered. "And our family life will be shattered."

"If it really bothers you, I won't argue about it tonight."

"Thank you." I turned to face the woods again as she entered the house. On impulse, I picked up my phone and pressed Cora Bellville's name.

It dialed briefly before a familiar voice picked up. "Hello, who is this? I lost all my contacts, so I don't know anyone's numbers..."

"Cora, it's me."

The other end was silent.

"Before you hang up, I just wanted to say I'm sorry. I was a jerk. I could give you millions of excuses, but they are just that: excuses. None of them excuse what I did. You don't have to forgive me. I understand if you don't..."

"Emily, please. Just don't. I really don't want to go through this. I got over it, okay? I'm fine now. I made new friends. I have a new life, and you didn't want to be in it. So, you're not. This conversation is pointless. We've both moved on." Her voice was harsh and unfamiliar.

I didn't say anything for a moment, but my voice cracked the minute I did. "Cora, I'm so sorry about your

Pops. He was like a grandfather to me. I miss him so incredibly much, and I can't imagine your pain."

"It was like losing two people at once." Her voice a hoarse whisper, but a familiar one.

"I am so *so* sorry." My voice was practically pleading.

"Me too."

It was silent for a moment. Then she hung up.

Waves of sorrow washed over me in varying levels of pain. It was the worst kind of sadness, one I couldn't blame on anyone but myself. Small drops from the sky began to wet my hair and my sketchbook beside me. Even as it began to storm, not a single breeze or gust touched my skin. Exhaling, I hunched over and grabbed my sketchbook, protecting it from the water falling slowly. My hands moved of their own accord, drawing the story my heart could not bear to tell me.

Chapter 39

The next morning, Luke and I planned to meet outside my house at eight. The morning birds were still chirping, and the sky was clear with a hint of a breeze, the perfect day for a hike. I woke up extra early to get ready and distract myself from thinking about last night's conversation. When I walked outside, I knew I looked good and tried not to blush when I felt Luke's eyes appraising me.

"What is all this?" He gestured toward what I was wearing.

My earlier excitement faded. "What do you mean?"

"We're going on a hike. You are dressed like you're going to a fancy gym or something. And why are you wearing makeup?"

I turned red. "I'm wearing exercise clothes."

"Why are you wearing makeup?"

"Why do you even care? It's only mascara from yesterday." *One little white lie is forgivable, right?*

"Whatever. Let's go."

I trudged behind him, trying to contain my anger. I took a deep breath to calm myself. "So, what's new in the world of Luke Wright?"

"Nothing really." He responded with little emotion.

Just continue normally. "I've noticed you and Harper have become friends again."

He snorted. "Sort of."

"Oh, well that's good."

"Why do you care?"

"I don't care. I was just trying to start a conversation." I was taken aback by his rudeness.

He stared straight ahead at the ground as we walked.

"Luke, is everything okay?"

"When is everything ever okay?"

This is so unlike Luke. "What's wrong?"

"It's nothing, okay?"

"Luke, I'm just trying to help."

"It's not like you tell me anything," he tossed back at me accusingly.

"That was months ago. I was going through a lot, and I made some mistakes. I'm sorry."

He stopped and turned to look at me. "Everything isn't just going to go back to how it used to be, you know. We got into a major fight a while ago, and we haven't talked in weeks. And now you're acting like everything is fine again."

I sucked in a tight breath of air. "I'm sorry. I totally get it. But I want to work through these things, so we can make everything fine again." *Please don't let us get into another fight.*

"Make what fine again?" His eyes were dark. "You know what I thought after I came to see your play? What is our friendship even based on? You said last time these hikes we go on our stupid. And you refused to talk to me about anything going on in your life."

"It's not true. I don't think our walks are stupid. I was angry, so I said something I didn't mean." I stopped and searched for words. "And I'm sorry I didn't tell you about what was going on. I didn't know how to tell you."

"Tell me what?" His expression was hard, but his eyes told a different story.

"My best friend from California's grandpa died. And I had kind of stopped talking to her over the summer because I was spending so much time with you."

His expression was still unforgiving.

My confidence was failing rapidly. "Talking to her was like being reminded over and over again of everything I missed in California. And it hurt too much. So, I stopped because it was the easy thing to do. I was wrong, and I made a mistake, and I lost a friend because of it." My words made the wound sitting on my heart much more real.

Lucas looked at me in disbelief. "So you abandoned her? Because missing home hurt too much?"

I was nearly at the point of tears. "This is why I didn't want to tell you. You wouldn't understand. You've never had to move away from home before and leave everything. I know I was wrong, but..."

He cut me off with a shake of his head. "I haven't moved, but I've been the one left. And it is so, *so* much worse."

I hated the way he looked at me, like I was everything wrong with the world.

"Luke, please. This is why I didn't want to tell you. I made a huge mistake, and it was hard for me to talk about."

"It should be hard for you to talk about." He sighed in disgust. "I can't believe it. This is so much worse than I thought." Luke turned away from me and ran his fingers through his hair, his whole body tense.

"Can we at least talk about it?"

"What is there to talk about?"

"What do you mean? This doesn't really have anything to do with you," I shot back.

"It has everything to do with me," he yelled. "How am I supposed to trust you to be a good friend after hearing this?"

"It was a completely different situation. Cora and I live thousands of miles apart, and there were a lot of other circumstances at play." At this point, I was practically pleading with him.

He shook his head and refused to respond.

"Why is this making you so angry?" I whispered. "I don't understand why this is affecting you so much."

He looked back at me with eyes I couldn't read. His voice was quiet this time. "Because I missed you too much when you weren't a part of my life. And it felt like—" He struggled for words. "It felt like it did when my sister left, except much different. I don't ever want to feel like that again."

"Luke, I'm not going to leave you."

"How am I supposed to trust you? First, my mother left. Then my sister. You left your other friend, and then you left me. How am I supposed to trust anybody?" He looked at me with eyes overflowing with hurt and confusion. "It's just not worth it anymore."

"So what are you going to do? Are you going to leave me now? You can't just go through life not trusting anyone. And you also can't put this all on me. This is something we have to work through together." My heart ached for him, but inside I was also screaming with frustration.

"I don't know what I'm going to do," Luke burst out. "I don't know," he repeated more quietly. "I just need some time."

I tried to hold in a sob, and watched him go again, too drained to think, even to feel. As I began to head back home, a thorn from a nearby bush tore into my skin, leaving an angry red scratch in its wake.

Chapter 40

He didn't answer my text that night, or the next day. He barely acknowledged me in the hallways, and we didn't see each other outside of school.

The winds grew icy cold those first few days, and the first snow fell the next week. No longer was the wind a cool companion. Instead, it was a harsh force. It blasted through my heavy coats and sent shivers down my spine whenever I walked outside. The rest of my first winter in Montana was brutal, and I missed California more than ever. Stuck inside constantly, I was often alone with my thoughts. On the edge of my consciousness always, guilt thinking about Cora haunted me especially when I was the loneliest. *Sometimes it's like she's a ghost or something.*

Chapter 41

"What are you up to, Emmy?"

I looked up with a tired smile at the familiar voice. It was nice to hear my dad talking to me, as his work had kept him busy for a while. "Just sketching."

The blueish rings below his warm brown eyes told the story of his exhaustion clearly. But even they could not distract me from the concern in his gaze. "Has everything been all right, hon?"

"Why do you ask?" I tried to look unperturbed as I continued with my drawing.

"I can't help but notice that you've been down a lot lately, and I was wondering, if you don't mind sharing, what's causing it?"

I let out a long breath, finding it easier to be more honest with him than anyone else in my family. "You're right. I have been down a lot lately."

His eyebrows furrowed, but his steady gaze urged me to continue.

The words left my mouth before I had time to think through them. "Dad, have you ever felt the kind of dissatisfaction that weighs on your mind, and your heart, and your stomach constantly? It's like an ache that never goes away except I really can't pinpoint the cause. I have a good life, a good family, no real reason to be dissatisfied. It permeates everything I do, turning even the brightest of days purplish-blue." *Not unlike the color of the circles underneath your own eyes.*

"And you have no idea what's causing it?"

The strongest reasons, Cora and Luke, I kept close to myself. "I have a small idea of some of it. But either there are so many little causes I can't find them all and root them out, or there is a large, overlying one, and it's too great to grasp. I'm too tired to sort it all through my mind." I looked up as I felt his strong arms suddenly encircle me. I let out another exhale, and when my voice escaped again, it was very small. "I'm so tired all the time."

He sat down next to me and looked me straight in the eye. "I just want you to know how proud I have been of you these past few weeks, throwing yourself into the play and everything else with the effort you have. It takes a lot of courage for quieter people like us to completely involve ourselves in an unfamiliar place, but you certainly did." A glint of humor shone in his otherwise troubled eyes. "Mom and Lydia like to rag on us all the time about getting more involved, but the two of them just blab so much it's easier for them to do whatever they want."

I laughed with him, but the sound was hollow.

"I say this in all seriousness. First, family is constant. No matter how troubled it may be or how troubled the world around it is, we are there for each other even when the world is not there for us. And secondly, you've engaged so fully in high school, and I'm proud of you. But don't forget the old you, which you seem to have tried to leave behind in California. It's perfectly normal to change, but always take the best parts with you lest you find yourself confused and dissatisfied in who you have become. When you truly know yourself, the problems around you are solved much more easily." He kissed the top of my head. "Don't forget you're still my little girl, no matter how grown up you think you are traipsing around with that dumb boy."

"Dad." I laughed.

"Shh, I'm not finished. Don't leave my little girl behind completely. And remember your friends in California. They'll keep you close to the core of who you are. For as good as the new is, you can never leave the old completely behind without consequences. I think you may have come to realize this."

Tears streamed steadily down my face. "But Dad, this is just so hard."

"You'll come through. You always do." He hugged me tighter still. "I love you, Emmy."

"I love you, too."

Even though I knew he was right, his answers were more troubling than the others I had already received and come to conclude myself. Like the rest of my problems, I shoved them away to the back recesses of my mind.

Chapter 42

Mom looked up in surprise from the sink when I walked through the door. "You're home earlier than usual."

"They let us out early because there's supposed to be a storm tonight," I muttered.

"How was school today?" She smiled at me as she finished wiping down the last dish and came over to give me a hug.

"Terrible, as usual."

"Oh honey, did something happen?"

"Everything is awful. It's been the same for weeks now. I missed the stupid tryouts for soccer. The play's over now. I barely have any friends." *I miss my old ones. I miss Cora. I miss Luke.* "I'm tired all the time. Emotionally tired. I hate this place." I couldn't keep the anger out of my tone as I started undoing my coat. A lump began to form in my throat. "I just want to go home."

I tried to continue on to my room, but my mom forced me to sit next to her at the kitchen table. "Emily, when we moved here, we knew it wouldn't be easy. I know it's hard. I know you miss your friends. We all do. But you also have to put some effort into this."

"I can't bloom like you want us to if there is no sun."

"What do you mean?" My mom's forehead wrinkled in worry.

"There's a snowstorm going on outside. There's no sun."

"Funny." She wasn't laughing.

"Mom, of course, that's not what I meant. I meant how are we supposed to bloom if there is nothing happy in our lives?" I stood up angrily and knocked the chair aside.

"Emily, come back here right now."

"I'm going to my room." As I ran up the stairs, I heard Lydia walk into the house, and the sounds of raised voices were telltale signs of yet another storm brewing in our house.

Chapter 43

The only sound at the dinner table was of silverware hitting plates. My mother's eyes were swollen from crying. Liam listlessly pushed his food around his plate with a frightened puppy-dog look on his face like always when people were fighting. Lydia angrily spooned food into her mouth, while my dad paced back and forth in the other room on the phone. As soon as he walked in and sat down, Lydia stood up.

"You know what, Mom? I can't keep my mouth shut anymore. I come home bearing news of my college acceptance into my number one choice, NYU, which also happens to be a highly selective school, and you started crying and getting angry over because I'm excited to leave home."

"And so round two begins," Liam mumbles quietly so only Dad and I can hear.

"How did you think I would react when you came home waving a letter in my face talking about how excited you were to leave this place you hate? I think 'hellhole' was the word you used. Did you once stop to think how hard I've worked to make this 'hated place' our home?" Mom's hands clutched her spoon.

Dad set his silverware down. "And I thought we'd have a nice, normal family dinner." He sighed. "What happened?"

"I was accepted into NYU's extremely selective drama program today in early admission. They even offered me quite a bit of money. I came home, expecting to be congratulated. This was not the case." She glared at Mom.

All of a sudden, Dad tuned in. "An acting program?"

"Yeah. I've decided it's what I want to do. When I'm through with college, I'll move out to LA, get an internship, and start auditioning."

"Lydia, you can't be serious." My mother covered her mouth with a hand. "I thought acting was just a hobby. NYU is so far away."

"You didn't think I was going to go to school in Montana, did you?" Lydia's eyes blazed. "No, acting isn't a hobby. I want to live in California, and Hollywood is pretty close to home."

Dad ran his hands through his hair. "Lydia, this is a serious decision. I don't think you've thought this through. Acting isn't a stable profession. It's almost impossible to make money and have a good career. You don't just walk into Hollywood and get cast as a leading lady. You have great potential. Your test scores show you can do anything you put your mind to. Please, don't waste it by trying to become a movie star."

"The day you guys factored us out of the equation when you decided to pack up and leave for the middle of nowhere was the day your input was factored out of my life decisions."

My dad's voice grew deadly serious. "We are your parents. As long as we are supporting you, you will receive our input, and you will listen to our decisions."

"Lydia, the decision to move here was a family decision..."

She cut Mom off with an angry glare. "Mom, it wasn't a family decision. You and Dad made the decision without consulting us. You simply announced we were moving without asking for our input. The last thing I want to hear is your speech about why we moved here. You may have power in many other aspects of my life, but I will choose where I am going to college. And I'm going to NYU." She turned and stormed up the stairs, shaking the house with every step and the final slam of her door.

Mom's hands covered her face and her whole body shook with silent sobs. My dad absently put a hand on her shoulder while he looked out the window with a clenched jaw. None of us moved for a while. Lydia was the blazing fire that melded us all together, or tore us all apart. Right now, her flames seemed to be burning us up. And nobody, not even Mom, dared to attempt to fight the fire when she was in a mood like this.

Chapter 44

Lydia was increasingly hostile, her mind far away. I, of course, was left alone.

This Monday afternoon was like any other for me. I moped around, alone in my room, sketching the icy turmoil outside my window. I suddenly heard loud footsteps outside my door and turned to see my mother's dark expression as she burst in. "Emily Elizabeth Lawrence. Would you care to explain this to me?" Her voice was angry but controlled as she held up a report card.

I rolled my eyes and continued my sketch. "What is there to explain?"

She swiftly walked over and abruptly closed the sketchbook. "Stop this attitude immediately, and look me in the eye."

I mocked her tone. "And what if I don't?"

"You won't play next season, and I'll take your phone away."

That shut me up. "Fine. What do you want me to say? I'm stupid? I'm not as smart as Lydia? I'm the talentless child? I can't get into college with those grades?"

"This is not the response I was looking for, and you know it. You are not stupid. You are much smarter than this, though I know high school is harder than middle school. You have a C- in math, Cs in English and science, a B- in Spanish and history, and one A in art. This is completely unacceptable, and you know it. I am not the kind of mother who checks my kids' grades constantly because I trusted you to handle your own work, but now it looks like I'm going to have to intervene. I am scheduling meetings with all your teachers, and we are going to discuss ways in which you are going to improve your study habits. Until you get your grades up, I'm taking away your phone and grounding you." Mom's cheeks were red with anger.

Out of the corner of my eye, I noticed Liam peeking in with wide eyes. "Well, Lydia's going to be an actress. Why can't I be an artist?" I was shaking. I was so upset at her inflammatory and pointed language directed at me. Suddenly, I realized my mom's hands were white and clenched. Tears began to flow down her cheeks, but she tried to smile through them.

"Emily, you can be anything you want to be. *Anything.* But your grades matter now. Your mind can change a lot in four years. When you're Lydia's age applying to college, I don't want you to regret the choices you make now because they *matter.* And *you* matter to me. Ultimately, your grades don't matter, nor does the college you go to, or the kind of job you get. Like any parent, I just want my kids to be happy. The reason your grades are important now is because they limit the choices you will have someday. Darling, I want you to have all the choices in the world." She wiped at her eyes and gave a small laugh. "I'm sorry for overreacting like this. Moms aren't supposed to cry."

Her fingers ran over the small sketchbook on my desk. Finally, she opened it to a random page. The rough sketch showed the beach and the ocean when it stormed. From the placement of the lifeguard towers and the rocks in the water, it was very obviously our beach, the one we had grown up going to. In the drawing, you could barely see a girl standing on a rock in the distance, her hands on her hips facing away from the sea while in the foreground was a younger girl facing the older one while a wave seemed caught in midair before it crashed on top of her.

"This is beautiful," Mom whispered.

Lydia suddenly appeared in the doorway, but at the sight of Mom's tear-streaked face and eyes as she looked at my drawing, she became still.

"When we moved here, I only wanted you kids to be happy—to enjoy what was left of your childhoods. The time goes so fast. I wanted you to learn to recognize the beauty in the simple things, in family, in nature, in each other. We only have one year, six months really, for all of us to be together. Then this time will be over. It'll be gone, and it won't come back. I didn't want us to waste them." She pulled a tissue from the box on my desk and dabbed at her eyes.

"I'm not perfect, and I made some mistakes. Because I'm a parent, my mistakes seem to have exponentially greater consequences because they affect you. When Dad and I made the decision to move, we thought it was the best decision for our family. Now, I'm not so sure. I knew it would be hard. Just not this hard. Please believe, it hasn't been easy for me either. These changes have been as hard for me as they were for you. Do you think I haven't missed my book club? All my friends? A home I loved, and activities I enjoyed? I thought I did it for all of us. I am so sorry for the pain this journey has caused you." Tears rolled down her cheeks again as she turned to face Liam and Lydia in the doorway. "I never wanted it to."

She sniffed. "Though you make fun of me for all my talk about blooming, I really wanted you to bloom. I thought this experience would give you perspective, a chance to restart, to grow as people, to understand a different way of life than our entitled one in California. While it will always be the place you want to go back to in your heart of hearts, home is where your family is. This piece of land, these gorgeous trees, this 'Dungeon Hill,' this creaky, wooden house, this is my home because you're here."

She turned to face my sister. "Lydia, when you leave for college, a part of my home goes with you wherever you go." The tears continued to roll down her cheeks. She sat down on my bed taking the notebook with her. "Are these all sketches of California?"

I nodded my head.

"Honey, these are beautiful." She laughed suddenly as she flipped through the pages and clapped her hand to her mouth. "Wilfred. Do you remember Wilfred, the grumpy old rabbit we had when you were little? Emmy, I had no idea you remembered him."

"Of course I remember Wilfred."

"Who gave him the strange name?"

Lydia raised her hand reluctantly. "Guilty as charged."

Liam took a step into the room. "It probably came from those strange books she always reads."

We giggled. Soon we sat together, looking at all the simple pictures, laughing and crying in turn. Then we brought out the photo albums, followed by our home videos.

By the time Dad came home, we were a crying, laughing mess.

"Well this is certainly not what I expected." He held up his hands. "No complaints from me." He was soon sitting on the ground with us going through everything all over again.

Finally, as we got ready to all go to bed, I saw Lydia reach over and put an arm around Mom. "You know, Mom, we are going to work through this. It'll take time, like things always do, but we'll figure it out."

And as she always did, Lydia managed to mend what she had broken apart.

Chapter 45

While occasional fights still broke out at home, it became a refuge for all of us. We were a team, for better or for worse, facing both the large and small challenges Montana presented.

I became more involved at school. I sat with Jacob and his friends at lunch, and hung out with the theater kids after classes ended. With some semblance of normality, I was able to push aside some of the hollowness, which still remained deep inside. However, forgetting was never an option. The guilt at the thought of Cora gradually dulled until it became slightly bearable. While my heart still ached at the sight of Luke in the hallways, his eyes never turned my way. I was afraid we were through forever.

Chapter 46

The sound of my phone vibrating woke me from my reverie on the front porch steps. The morning air was cool, but not unbearable. I was blissfully alone. Not intending to answer it, I glanced down out of curiosity to see the caller ID. The name on it immediately started my heart pumping.

My hand shook as I answered the call. "Hello?"

"Emily?"

"Yeah it's me."

"It's Cora."

"I know."

Her voice was quiet. "Carter asked me out yesterday."

I squealed. "Carter? *The* Carter?" Cora had been practically in love with this guy for as long as I could remember.

Her breath released in a whoosh. "Yes. I couldn't believe it." Cora was quiet for a second. "And after it happened, I realized the only one I wanted to talk to about it was you."

I had no idea what to say so I stayed silent.

"I don't have my life together like I said. I barely have any friends left because I've been so miserable. You are my oldest friend, my closest friend, and the person I want to talk to whenever I have anything meaningful to say. I've missed you." A soft sob sounded over the line.

"I've missed you, too." Those words were all I needed to say. We shared a moment of contented silence.

Then I looked up to see a young woman standing on the porch. I guessed she was no older than twenty-three or twenty-four. She wore jeans and a big jacket, but she looked as though she would be just as at ease in a business suit.

"Um, Cora? Can I call you back, and we can catch up? I want to hear everything, but someone is here, and I have to answer the door. I'll explain later."

Her acknowledgement was all I needed to hear. I quickly hung up and greeted the stranger.

"Hello." I could barely focus on her with warmth and peace permeating every cell in my body. *Girls certainly have a remarkable way of tearing each other down, but somehow, we always pick up our broken pieces enough to put others back together as well.*

"Hi. I'm looking for the Lawrence family." Her words snapped me back to reality. The girl's features were average with nothing notable except her eyes. They stood out like sparkling jewels and drew me in with warmth. Yet, the intelligence I saw there intimidated me.

"Uh, yes, I'm Emily Lawrence." I suddenly felt embarrassed about my appearance. "I'm sorry I look so terrible. I just woke up, but the rest of my family is still asleep. Would you rather come back later when they're' awake?" I suddenly realized I didn't even know who she was. "Um, also I didn't catch your name...."

"Oh of course. I'm Emily too, actually. Emily Wright. I think you know my brother." She smiled. "I came at the perfect time actually, because you're the person I came to see."

"Oh." I stood at the door feeling shell-shocked. "Let me grab a jacket and shoes. It's kind of a nice morning. Do you want to go for a walk? I'd rather not wake everyone else up."

"Perfect. I'll wait out here."

I ran upstairs, changed into jeans, grabbed my biggest jacket and boots and joined Emily Wright outside.

The snow crunched loudly as we walked in silence for a few moments.

"You're probably wondering why I came to see you, right?"

I nodded. "To be honest, I didn't think you knew who I was."

"Yes, well, when I arrived yesterday from the east coast, we drove by here. My dad told me someone had finally moved into this old place. I was planning on coming to meet your family this morning, and Dad told me you and Luke were good friends."

"Yeah, at least we used to be." I kicked up some snow with my toe.

She sighed, and her eyebrows furrowed as she looked out into the trees. "So, he hasn't grown out of it."

I looked up in surprise. "Grown out of what?"

"He's done this ever since we were kids. He's so scared of people leaving him, he pushes them away before they can leave by themselves. I watched him do it for years." She laughed, but I could hear brokenness in it. "Until he pushed me away, too."

We both pondered her words in silence as we walked along a path in the snow, lined by thick trees. Even with winter's white coat covering it, I recognized the trail. We approached the creek, now frozen solid. The sun's morning rays shimmered off the ice.

"Emily's Creek," I whispered and attempted a smile.

She looked at me curiously and then back at the stream. "I didn't realize he gave it a name."

"He said he named it after you."

"He never used it when we used to come here. I think he named it after both the Emilys in his life."

"I wouldn't say I'm a part of his life anymore." I reached down and grabbed a handful of snow with my gloved hands. "He's shut me out for good, I think."

"Trust me, I understand. I'm his sister."

"Why did he...um...push you away as you put it? If you don't mind my asking—"

"When he was a little kid, he made me promise we would always be friends and always be close. He took the last part literally. When my mother died, he became my responsibility. I also had a goal to fulfill her dreams, go to college, live in a big city, have a career. So I did. We each take a different path to find ourselves, to find the pieces we've lost." She sighed.

"This was the spot where I told him I was going away to college. He didn't take it well." She walked over to sit on a big rock next to the creek and let her legs dangle over the frozen water. For a moment, I caught a glimpse of the girl she used to be. I could imagine her sitting in the exact spot talking and laughing with a small Lucas as he jumped around the flowing water, tossing sticks, and watching them race downstream. "But I had to go. I had been a mother to him, a caretaker for my father, the housekeeper, and then a sister and a daughter all in one. I loved it, but I was also exhausted. I needed to find my way in a world outside our small house in the Montana forest."

She didn't talk for a while, perhaps remembering those days. She took a deep breath. "When I was leaving, he told me I was breaking the pact we had made, that I was abandoning him. I told him we could still be close, even if I lived far away. I tried to convince him being close meant connected in our hearts. He was angry and told me never to come back unless I came back to stay. It was the last time he talked to me. He refused to leave his room to say goodbye the day I left. Since then, he's refused to answer my calls, cards, email, and texts."

My heart ached for her. "I'm so sorry."

"It's my fault. I should have realized he needed me. He was only twelve when I left after all, but I had been there for him all my life. I thought I needed a break to live my own life like I always dreamed I would. I wanted to come back to visit, but I knew I couldn't stay like Luke wanted me to. Things couldn't go back to the way they had been. But, I've missed Dad and Luke too much to stay away any longer. I realize I made a mistake by not coming back to visit sooner." Her voice carried through the woods surrounding us.

"I came home as soon as my semester ended because Dad said Luke needed me." She sighed. "But he won't talk to me. This morning, I took an early walk through the woods. It's been a long time since I've been to all my childhood haunts. They told me something I've needed to hear for a long time."

"And what was that?" I prompted her.

"It's time for me to come home to stay, but it's going to be different this time. I know Luke needs me, more than he admits, but what I didn't realize until this morning was I needed home more. I chased the city and my mother's dreams, hoping to find her. But I really just chased a ghost. Mom wasn't in the city, or medical school or living a fast-paced life. She was here all along, in Luke and Dad. Of course, I can't explain all this to him because he's avoiding me. So, I came to you. Dad told me you were the first person to make my brother happy in a long time."

"But he has so many friends, Lucy, Jack, Matt, and the rest of the group."

"He's known those kids since they were three. Our moms were all friends. He pretends they're all still close. In reality, Dad says he barely talks to them or hangs out with them. Dad told me you were different."

I shrugged off her last remark. "He had a girlfriend for a while, Harper. They must have been close. I think they're still friends, actually."

Her face darkened. "A lot of not-so-nice names come to mind for her. Dad told me all about her. She wanted a cute boyfriend. Luke was trying to fill a hole in his life. Obviously, it worked out well." Her voice dripped with sarcasm. "No, you were different, all right."

My heart constricted more than I thought possible. "If I was so different, why did he push me away? I know I made mistakes. I know I should have known better than to let my feelings get the best of me. I should have realized he never could have felt anything more than friendship for me, but I tried. I honestly did. I loved him as my friend, but when I needed him, I didn't know where he was."

I closed my eyes tightly to reorient and distract myself from rising emotion. "I don't even know what I'm doing right now. I'm out in the wilderness with Luke's sister. Luke, the guy who sent me into depression for weeks, who hasn't spoken to me in months. All of this brings back painful emotions I thought I had dealt with." I swallowed back the lump in my throat. "I don't even know why I'm telling you this. I just met you this morning." I tried to smile. "Honestly though, I feel like I've known you for a lot longer. Lucas talked about you once in a while. Maybe I'm ranting because you're the only other person I've met who understands what I'm going through."

The other Emily looked off in the distance. "Losing a parent can affect a kid a lot. God only knows how much it's affected me, but everyone who loses a person they love must reach a point where they stop letting their grief control their actions."

"Lucas said your mom died when he was little, right?"

She shrugged. "He was three and too young to remember her, but he missed having her in his life. He grieved when I left because he thought he was losing me, too. Now, he seems to be grieving because he thinks he's lost you." She paused and raised her voice to a higher volume.

What is she doing that for?

"What he needs to learn is to stop giving up on people so easily. He needs to learn to let them go without thinking he's lost them. You only truly lose a person when you give up on them. I haven't given up on my mother. She's still with me. Even though you gave up on me, Lucas, I was still with you because I didn't give up on you, I didn't let you go." She paused to let her voice echo through the trees. "So, are you ready to come out now? I know you're there."

I froze. "What are you talking about? Has Luke been here the whole time?" My voice faded away in shock.

She stood up, and I followed her through a tiny opening in a thick bush. "Right behind here. Didn't you ever show her this, little bro? This is called Luke's Creek."

As soon as I pushed through the dense brush, the first thing my eyes found was Luke, standing motionless and speechless on the other side of a small stream. His sister stood opposite him.

"How did you know I was here?" Luke looked down at the snow under his feet.

"I knew the whole time. I can sense your presence from a mile away." She laughed. "Just kidding. You left footprints everywhere, you dingo. It was the first thing I taught you about hiding and tracking in the snow: never leave footprints. Looks like you need a refresher." Her voice softened. "What do you say to a refresher course this afternoon?"

In a single leap, he bounded over the stream and straight into his sister's arms. Finally, he pulled back. "Why didn't you tell me to come out earlier or tell me you knew I was here?" He dared a small glance at me before looking away.

I felt uncomfortable, like I was intruding on an intimate moment.

"Because I knew you wouldn't listen to me any other way. You may be bigger and stronger than I am now, but I will always outsmart you."

"Why can't we do the refresher course now?" It was strange to see this new side of Lucas. He was like an eager little boy again with his older sister.

She shook her head. "I think you and this other Emily have some talking to do."

He looked at me for a while with an expression I couldn't quite discern. Finally, he nodded his head and smiled before turning back to look at his sister. "Are you really back, for good I mean?"

She hugged him again. "For good." She went on her tiptoes to whisper something in his ear, and his face turned red.

She whispered something else.

My face grew warm, and I tried to look away.

He looked at me and blushed again, and then muttered something back.

She slapped him lightly on the back and shoved him toward me. "Go, be a man for once."

I thought at this point I was as close to dying of humiliation as I had ever been.

"I'll be at the house. It was nice meeting you, Emily." She turned and walked away.

Luke and I stood awkwardly for a moment before he broke the silence. "Hi."

"Hi." I shivered in the light morning breeze. We were quiet for a moment, soaking in the comfort of the rare warm wind and unsure of what to say.

"Well, you've met my sister. She pulls tricks on me like that all the time." He smiled affectionately.

I laughed. "I don't think it was a trick. It was a well-thought-out plot against us."

He chuckled but sobered quickly. He shoved his hands nervously into his pocket. "Can I show you something?"

"Sure."

"Back a couple of miles, the Emily and Luke Creeks are one river, but they split because a big log fell in the middle a long time ago." He walked a bit and stopped. "Down here is where they meet again. I call it the Right River."

"W-r-i-g-h-t River, as in your last name? Very creative."

"No, Right River. R-i-g-h-t River. Because the Emily and Luke streams are supposed to be connected. It's the right way they were meant to be."

I gave him a look, which clearly said, "You'll have to do better."

"Emily, what I'm trying to say is I'm sorry. I messed this up. I tried so hard not to lose you, to keep myself from getting too attached, I ended up pushing you away. In the process, I got myself really lost. You heard my sister. She had to come back home because I was such a mess."

"I was the one who wasn't supposed to fall in love with you." I looked at the ground and then into his eyes.

He stepped closer to me. "Yeah, well I should have taken my own advice because I fell in love with you first."

I sucked a deep breath of air in shock.

He laughed at what must have been my dumbfounded expression. He took another step closer. His hand touched my cheek. "Can I try again?"

I barely had time to nod before he was kissing me. As he gently pulled away, I opened my eyes only to see we were standing at the exact spot where the Lucas and Emily streams met again.

Epilogue

Our hair was tangled in the vibrant green grass of late spring as we quietly rested on the soft ground. My sketchbook lay just inches away, abandoned when Luke had interrupted my quiet afternoon. The warm breeze whipped its pages around, and just as quickly travelled all over me and sent my hair flying over Luke's face. I closed my eyes, mesmerized by the delicious shivers running down my spine and the goosebumps covering my bare arms. In my reverie, it was all too easy to ignore Luke's muttering about the annoying breeze, which made my hair tickle his face.

"Can we please go sit on the fence? The grass is starting to make my legs itch."

His pointed question was more difficult to ignore. I sighed. "The fence is getting so old. It could break at any second with the two of us sitting on it. You're the one who interrupted my quiet afternoon, so you don't get to set the agenda."

He snorted. "What agenda? We're lying on the ground in the middle of a massive meadow without talking."

"I would prefer to say we are contemplating the complexities of life by focusing on the simple beauty of the world around us."

"I have no idea how you got that idea from us sitting here trying not to itch our skin while bugs crawl all over us."

I rolled my eyes. "Luke, just close your eyes. Appreciate the breeze. Smell the little wildflowers all around us."

"Why do you like this place so much again?"

"It's my thinking meadow."

"And what is it you're thinking about right now?"

"Well because you keep interrupting me, I'm thinking about how unfortunate it was that I chose this particular spot to be my thinking place four years ago. If I hadn't, I wouldn't be hearing you complain."

His tone contained mock indignation. "Complain? Me complain? Never. I am just remarking on the unfortunate thinking place you decided on." He adjusted himself on the ground, rolling over onto his side.

I couldn't help but laugh. "Whatever." I rolled over to face the same direction, curious as to what he was looking at. *A leaf. How am I not surprised?* His birthmark peeked out of the top of his shirt, and my fingers absentmindedly reached up to touch it.

"So what'll it be? Storm cloud or fluffy cloud?" His voice broke the quiet again.

"It's a wind cloud."

"What the heck is that?"

"It's a cloud, which always travels with the wind."

"Ah, so we are playing the metaphor game. And what are you, the wind?"

I laughed. "Maybe."

Ding. I slowly pulled out my phone and laughed when I saw the text.

i found something even better than arguing

Along with the caption, Lydia had sent me a picture of her with a poster in hand surrounded by protesters on some street in New York with Finn right at her side. *I'm so happy they found each other again.*

I laughed and showed Luke. "I think Lydia's found her calling."

"Something better than arguing? I didn't know it was possible for her."

"She'll get a degree in law along with one in drama." I soaked in the warm air for another moment. "I miss seeing her so much. I can't believe she only has one more year before she graduates from college."

He laughed. "*You* graduate from high school tomorrow. Now that's crazy."

I shuddered at the thought. "It's so weird. I know it's cliché, but it feels like yesterday I was in this very same meadow, a little fifteen-year-old who had just moved from California. I had no idea who I was. I missed home so desperately I didn't even know what to do with myself. And in this same meadow you walked into my life."

He chuckled. "And you were love-struck the moment you saw me."

I laughed. "Yes, but it's not the point. The point is tomorrow I graduate. I turn nineteen in a month. And in three months, I head off to college back in California. Sometimes I still feel fifteen." I sighed. "How can I be old enough to go to college? I don't think I'm ready." I couldn't voice the thoughts weighing on me the most. *I'm not ready to leave my family. But, I don't think I'm ready to leave Luke.*

"You'll be all right. Besides, Cora is going to college right around the corner from you. Your respective roommates are going to hate you because the two of you are going to be hanging out in each other's dorms all the time. And Lydia will be only a few hours away at UCLA getting her graduate degree."

"I'm looking forward to it." I couldn't keep the hint of sadness out of my tone. "Are you going to miss me from here in Montana?" Luke still hadn't told me which university he was planning to transfer to after he had finished community college this spring, but I knew his goal had always been to go somewhere near his dad.

He smiled. "I won't have to."

I sat up. "What?"

"I'm going to school in California."

"Luke. But going to school around here was your dream. What about your dad?"

"Dreams change. I think the best thing for me is to get a fresh perspective and see the outside world a little bit before I decide to settle down here for the rest of my life. My sister's medical school is just forty-five minutes away, so she'll be able to keep an eye on him. Besides, she's hoping to get a residency even closer when she finishes."

I squealed and hugged him, burying my face in his shoulder. "I'm so happy right now I could burst."

"Well let's not do that," he commented drily. He sobered. "But it isn't going to be exactly the same, Ems."

"I know. Life is always different when you move on to the next phase. You just have to take the best parts with you."

He smiled and started to brush himself off.

"Where are you going?"

"I have to go find my suit for your graduation tomorrow."

"You're coming?"

"Always the tone of surprise." He laughed. "You think I'm going to college in California in part to be near you, but I wouldn't go to your graduation?"

I flushed and laughed with him. "I don't know what I was thinking."

He kissed me goodbye, and I watched as he walked away with his hands in his pockets, disappearing into the woods with the breeze tousling his hair as he walked.

I turned and leaned back on my elbows, facing the hill with my home perched on top. *Soon it'll be my old home.* A familiar ache twinged my heart, and this time I welcomed it like an old friend. *At least this time I know to take the best parts with me. Cora's there waiting. And Luke will be with me.* I exhaled and rested on my back. My eyes glanced up past the towering trees, which lined the meadow, to the blue sky beyond. *I can't remember if the sky is this blue in California.* I smiled as the clouds distracted me from these thoughts. They slowly but surely made their way across the expanse, carried along by the imperceptible breeze. It must have heard me thinking, for the wind travelled down, swirling around, and wrapping me in its warm embrace. *Even thousands of miles away in California, there will always be the same wind.*

Dear Reader,

After spending my life reading historical fiction, biographies, classics, and the occasional Harry Potter reread, it is mildly shocking to me that my first published book turned out to be a young adult coming-of-age and romance novel. This book began as the small fantasy of a fourteen-year-old me, and somehow it miraculously turned into a novel. As much fun as it was to write, it is certainly not a genre I ever imagined myself writing. In the future, I look forward to writing projects in a variety of genres.

Even so, I am incredibly excited to have been able to share with you the result of many hundreds of hours of writing and editing. This book does not contain the depth of classic literature, but if my words brought you a smile, a memory, or a laugh, I will have done my job.

Writing is always a work in progress. I would love to hear your comments or thoughts on *Trust the Wind*. I am currently working on a poetry book and another novel, so please keep in touch with my periodic updates. I post regularly on my blog and social media platforms.

Thank you for coming on this journey with me. Your support through simply reading this novel means more then you will ever know. You have made the longtime dream of a young, book-loving romantic come true.

Sincerely,
Claire Crafts

Acknowledgements

I am mildly overwhelmed as I begin writing this section because so many people made this book possible. Of course, I have to begin with the people who truly brought this dream to culmination: my writing parents, Lorna and Larry Collins. Lorna, without your constant encouragement, advice, and editing, I would never have made it to this point. Your mentorship means the world to me. Larry, thank you for always keeping a smile on our faces throughout this entire process and designing the beautiful cover art.

I also would be extremely remiss if I didn't thank my wonderful parents, who have encouraged me and supported me through many years of writing. Thanks as well to my siblings for the comic relief and the friendly teasing which kept my head from being in the clouds of Montana all the time. I'm so glad to be able to call all of you my family.

Thank you also to my beautiful friends who kept me from being *too* nerdy and always manage to keep me sane. You guys know who you are and have to also know by this point that you make my world a much better place. I'm very grateful to my Latin class for supporting me through this entire process and believing I could do this (well, some of you). I wasn't kidding when I said I was putting you in my book...

And finally, thank you to Lagunita Writers Group for sticking with me for over five years from the time I was a little girl of ten with a short story about a prairie. This wouldn't be what it is without you.

About the Author

Claire Crafts is a sixteen-year-old author and poet living in Orange County, California. Not so long ago, she was a young avid reader with a book in one hand and a dream in her heart. She is now absolutely thrilled to be able to present the culmination of this dream to you in the form of her first novel.

When she is not writing, she enjoys travelling, spending time with her friends and family, participating in far too many school activities, and of course, finding as much time as possible for reading.

Find her on Instagram: @clairecrafts and @seeking.extraordinary for writing updates
Blog: www.seekingextraordinary.weebly.com

Made in the USA
San Bernardino, CA
30 April 2018